DOUBLE DISCOVERY

SHADOWS OVER ELISTA, BOOK 1

CLARA WILS

Gryphon's Gate Publishing

Gryphon's Gate Publishing
550 King St. N.
PO Box 42088 Conestoga
Waterloo, ON
N2L 6K5

ISBN: 978-1-990587-08-5

CHAPTER 1

ASHA

"Are you certain you want to do this?" Tamia asked softly, hugging me close. "For someone who isn't looking for another commitment, this is a pretty big one."

True, but it wasn't like I was running off to marry another man. Bonding with a Lumani was vastly different. And I needed to do something to help me — hopefully — fill in the gaping hole in my life where Davas had been.

My soul ached to feel the wiry strength in his arms, the callouses on his hands, the stubble on his chin. But he'd been taken by the Dream Fever — as had so many others — this past winter. I had loved him with every speck of my being, and he was gone. I honestly didn't know if it would be possible for me to love anyone ever again, like I'd loved him. But perhaps Bonding with a Lumani spirit would help me to feel alive again.

Yet, there was no guarantee I'd even become one of the Chosen.

In truth, I didn't know what I wanted, but... this felt right. If I couldn't have my love, I'd dedicate myself in service to Elista. That seemed a fitting memorial for Davas.

But I couldn't tell Tamia what I was feeling, how lost and alone and hollow I felt. I don't think she understood why I couldn't stay here, in Bell Cove. Yes, I had family here, but now that Sala had left, it was only Tamia and me. That wasn't enough. There were too many memories here. Once they had filled my soul with joy, but now they were bitter-sweet and reminded me only of what I had lost.

"I'm certain," I lied to my sister.

In many ways she'd been more of a mother to me than a sister. Our mother had been past childbearing age — or so everyone had thought, until I'd come along — and had died giving birth to me. Our father had been lost at sea just a few months earlier. Tamia had been married with a baby of her own at that time, so I'd been given into her care as a newborn. She'd raised me as her own, alongside her daughter — my niece, though I thought of her as a sister — Sala.

I pulled back from our embrace to look at her. Despite the twenty years that separated us in age, we were very similar in look, Tamia and I. There was more gray in the waves of her dark auburn hair, and she was a bit heavier through her torso than I was. Otherwise, we were of a height with nearly identical builds, the same dark-honey skin, and large, sable-brown eyes. Some said she was the image of my mother at that age — which was nearly the age my mother was when I was born — and I could see the mother I should have had.

I smiled. "You've done so much for me, Tamia, but we both know if I don't do this... I'll just linger around your house and... dwindle. Sala is married and gone now." My "sister" had married just this past year, leaving Bell Cove for Moon Harbor to live with her new husband. "I need to do... something, and this will be my last chance to try the Choosing." I was twenty. If I wasn't Chosen this year, I'd be too old to go next year.

She smiled and nodded, a sad look in her eyes. "I know Asha, I know. I just... don't want to lose you." She let out a heavy sigh. "If you're Chosen, you'll be off doing important things. Meli's son was Chosen three years ago, and he hasn't been back since."

"I'll be back, I promise. I can't say when, but I'll be back."

"I know you will." Tamia drew herself up and put on a joyous smile, which I knew she wasn't feeling. "Then go, get in there, the Lumani are already arriving."

I turned to see the floating orbs of light beginning to filter over the crowd of young men and women. Turning back, I kissed the only mother I'd ever known on her cheek, then ran to join the others.

There weren't many in the crowd, despite the fact that the Choosing only came to Peter's Town every other year. Children from this area could travel up to Cragmount or east to Thalanford, in the other years. But, with the Dream Fever having taken the lives of so many children and adults this past winter, many were needed at home. As such, the crowd of youths gathered in the Peter's Town square was no more than twenty. That meant greater odds of being Chosen, even if only three Lumani had been brought to find new hosts.

I was a bit out of breath as I reached the small crowd, hoping I wasn't too late. The three Lumani were already hovering over three other hopefuls and I could hear one side of a few hushed conversations. I tried not to listen in. It wasn't my place. I just kept still and hoped, desperately, that one of those three wouldn't be Chosen and maybe...

A Lumani broke away from the young man they'd been hovering over and moved in my direction. I thought this one particularly beautiful. It was a smaller ball of constantly mixing pale blues and pinks, its colors clearly visible due to its less brilliant nature than the other two. The others were near to blinding: one a brilliant sun-yellow, the other near to white as far as I could tell.

What is your name? a voice spoke into my head. *I am Leoa.*

"Asha, your brilliance," I said with a reverent nod of my head. "I am honored by your presence." Those were the words I'd been told to say.

Leoa laughed, a full and melodic sound. *How very formal of you, Asha. That is a beautiful name, but you will be given a new one. It would be a shame to give up such a lovely name.*

I did love my name, I too thought it beautiful and so had the many who'd known me. And yet. "I know, Leoa," I said softly. "And perhaps I will be blessed with a second beautiful name." It was my turn to give a little laugh. "Or I might end up with a name like our current queen. Either way, I will accept it and love it, as it will mean I have been Chosen and am able to serve my nation."

Is that why you wish to Bond? To serve?

"Yes. I have always felt it my purpose to care for others." That was true. Even if I didn't really know why I wanted to Bond, I'd always been drawn to share the abundance of love in my heart and help others.

I can sense that about you, compassionate and gentle, caring and diligent. Would you say that describes you?

That would probably be how many back home would describe me, but for a Lumani to see that in me was quite humbling. "Yes, Leoa, thank you, I feel truly honored that you see such things in me."

And how would you wish to care for people, if you had your way?

"I... don't know yet."

You do not wish to bring comfort to just one, a true love?

And so Leoa had seen through to my heart. "No. I am blessed to have been given that opportunity and it was glorious and beautiful, but..." I had to stop as my voice was choking up, tears in my eyes as I recalled Davas.

You're so young, but... you truly loved him.

"Yes." I could say little more through my tears.

And if Chosen, you will give all your love to the nation instead?

"Yes."

There was a long pause before Leoa said softly. *It seems my companions have already Chosen.*

I hadn't been paying attention, lost in my own turbulent emotions.

I am touched by the depths of your love, young one. I have felt as you have for another only once, in all my lifetimes. It is a rare and precious gift. Your large heart calls to me. Shall we care for this nation together?

Leoa was asking me?

"Yes, that would be my dearest wish," I said, recovering from my grief.

Then consider yourself Chosen, Asha. Leoa floated down to my shoulder, settling there, and I felt a glorious warmth touch me. And as that warmth filled me and filtered down to my heart, I felt a connection, something grasped and held within me. I didn't know how, but I knew I'd be as close to this precious being of light as I'd ever been to Davas.

Oh.... I felt that, Leoa said softly. *Yes. I think we'll do well together, Asha. Come, this way.* Leoa left my shoulder and began floating away. I followed; entranced.

If you have any to whom you wish to say farewell, you should do so now.

I nodded. "Thank you, Leoa, I do."

Meet me by that third carriage, I'll wait there.

I broke away from Leoa and went to Tamia. She was practically quivering with joy. "I can't believe it! You were Chosen!"

"I know! Their name is Leoa, and they... they understand all these mixed-up feelings inside me. I think... I think they'll really help me."

We embraced again. "I'm so happy for you!" Tamia said. "Go out there and heal this world, Asha. It's what you've always done. You touch people's hearts and bring them to life."

I'd never heard her speak about me that way. I felt truly blessed in that moment. "Thank you, Mother... Sister," I said softly, on the verge of tears again.

She wept with me as we held each other, then walked me to the carriage. We embraced again and said our goodbyes before I rejoined Leoa and entered the carriage. We were far from Silverveil, so these were fast carriages, meant to get us to the school for Chosen — all the way on the other side of the Elista — in a little over a week.

I waved to Tamia as the carriage pulled away, then sat back on the cushioned seat, a little stunned.

How do you feel? Leoa asked.

I felt... so many things. "I feel... a bit lost, a bit surprised, a bit stunned. But also full of wonder." Having always been deeply in tune with my own emotions, I searched deeper within myself. "And, I'm terrified. I've never been this far from my home before, and I'm about to travel across the nation!" I smiled. "But I'm also excited and curious what the future will bring. I'm feeling so many things, but most of all I feel blessed."

Blessed?

"Yes, blessed." I settled, my emotions calming a little. "I've had a blessed life, with the chance to truly love someone. And now... it's like I'm starting a new life and this new opportunity is a blessing as well. One I truly needed, so, thank you Leoa. Thank you."

I think we shall both be blessed, Leoa said softly.

CHAPTER 2

DAWN

I felt a certain symmetry as I joined the crowd of young men and women in the large town square of Miraline. My mother had been Chosen in Miraline, and now here I was, at the same age, in the same place. Though... my parents had no clue I was here. I'd broken ties with them five years ago and disappeared. Ona Midnight had checked in on me now and then. She wasn't truly Ona, not related to me, but she was so close to my mother I felt like she was. But the last I'd seen of Midnight had been over three years ago, at a port city in Fiore. I'd been about to board a ship crossing the Austel Ocean. She'd said she couldn't follow me where I was going and bade me luck on my journey. I think she'd been trying to convince me to stay on the northern continent, but I couldn't. I'd needed to wander, to see as many places and peoples as I could.

Now... I'd done my wandering and had felt compelled to return home. And it had been just in time for my last chance at the Choosing. At twenty I'd not have been able to try again next year.

"What do we do?" Eadric asked next to me.

I sighed. I still couldn't believe he'd followed me this far. But I shouldn't have been surprised. He'd followed me across two continents and countless nations. But still... I didn't think he belonged at a Choosing. Would the Lumani even Choose a full-blooded Fey?

"I don't know what the process is. I plan on just sitting here. You can do as you like." That was usually my reply to him: *you can do as you like.* He was a good friend but looked to me for instruction just a little too often. I wasn't his keeper. I knew he wanted me to be his soul-bonded as the Fey called a spouse, but I wasn't ready for that. I didn't want to be limited to just one man... not yet anyways. For all my worldliness, I was vastly inexperienced in being... a woman. I'd been too busy seeing the wonders of this world to be with men, even one man, not even Eadric. He'd always been well with that. He'd offered once and I'd turned him down, and he'd never said anything about it again, but he'd stayed with me, to show me how much he wanted to be... close to me. Sometimes he could be sweet and endearing, mostly he was just annoying. Though... in truth, he was the only real friend I had. For all the interesting people I'd met, he was the only one I was close to.

My mother had had several lovers in addition to my father, a union all had agreed to, a sharing of love and an intimate family. And I was starting to feel that I might want to have something similar. That desire, more than anything else, was what had driven me home.

I wanted a deep connection. To explore what it was like to connect with people, physically and emotionally. That's what truly excited me. The Choosing itself, didn't matter. I'd find people to connect with whether or not I was Chosen. All the Choosing would do was get me into Silverveil, a good place to have a tryst or two, from what I'd heard.

So, since I didn't care about being Chosen or not, I sat and used one of Ona Ahmaia's meditation techniques to bring peace to my thoughts and emotions. I found stillness and serenity and sunk into it with a smile.

"They're coming," Eadric said next to me, still standing as far as I knew. "Ah... they're... they're all coming... this way."

That was intriguing, but I pushed the emotion down and found stillness again.

"Ah... Dawn... I think you should see this." The awe and overwhelm in Eadric's voice prompted me to look. I opened my eyes and gazed up to see more than a dozen Lumani all hovering over me.

Then they all began speaking into my mind at once.

Hello, who are you?

Your spirit is so strong and yet so still.

Do you not wish to be Chosen? Why...?

Who are you, young one?

Fascinating, I can feel...

And on and on they went.

With Ona Ahmaia's meditation, I was able to filter them out. Didn't they know I couldn't talk to them all at once? I'd let them figure out who would go first.

Oddly, it was a conversation outside of me, which caught my attention.

"Ah... yes, I am a Fey, and you are?" Eadric said. Since I couldn't hear the other side of the conversation, I assumed a Lumani was speaking to him.

"It is a pleasure to meet you, Eona. Can you tell me more of this Binding and Choosing? My companion has explained some of it to me, but I'd like to hear what you have to say about it." That was Eadric, always so precise and studious.

One of the voices within me caught my attention. It wasn't inundating me with questions and calls for attention like the others, instead... it was singing a lovely tune. I filtered through the many voices and selected just that one.

I spoke to it, in the same mind-voice. *That is a lovely tune, very soothing.* I said, curious.

Thank you, I used to sing it to my children in another life, a lullaby. I learned it from my host and found it to be, as you say, soothing and relaxing. The voice was masculine and strong, a serene tenor.

And why did you choose to sing it, instead of blasting me with words, like the others?

A faint laugh. *I sensed the immensity of peace within you. I, like the others, found the vastness of your spirit contrasted with the depth of this serenity to be an anomaly to investigate. Most young men and women are wracked with emotions of all sorts during the Choosing, but you are... still. I thought, perhaps a quiet and relaxing song might aid your stillness. Was I right?"*

You were, yes. Thank you. What is your name?

I am Amya, and you are?

Dawn.

Dawn... as in the daughter of our queen and heir to the Vauphan throne?

You are very astute, Amya. Yes.

Many have wondered why you have not appeared at a Choosing before now.

And they'll keep wondering until I wish to say something. But I'm not one to explain myself to others. I do as I wish. I suppose that is something you must know if you Choose to be with me. I will not be like any others. I will not change my name or bow to tradition. I go my own way and make my own mistakes. It's a rocky path, but I wouldn't have it any other way. I need to be free.

*Yes, I sensed that about you, the need for freedom, but also...
the headstrong, radical nature you possess.* A laugh. *I shouldn't
be surprised. Already you've turned this Choosing on its head. In
truth it will be you Choosing from us Lumani, not the other way
around, I think.*

*Indeed. And how would you feel about being Bonded to a
head-strong 'radical,' as you call me.* I liked that word, it
seemed to sum me up well.

*I have led many lives, some more adventurous than others,
but never... a radical life. That would be a new experience indeed.
It would be my honor to be Chosen by you.*

*You were different enough in getting my attention, sensing
what I needed. You're not like these others. I Choose you, Amya.*

And I you, Dawn.

Something must have happened between us, as the
other Lumani stopped chattering away within me and
began to disperse. Only two remained. Amya, floating above
me, and another next to Eadric.

I rose and held out my hand. Amya settled in my palm, a
large, warm ball of deep reds and fiery oranges. Yes, those
colors seemed to match my soul.

"I'm done," I said to Eadric and began to leave the crowd.

"I'll be there in a moment," he said, then continued his
conversation with his own Lumani. "Fascinating!" he said, as
I walked away, shaking my head.

Indeed, Eadric did find me at the line of carriages not
long later, his own ball of blue and green bobbing along
beside him. I was just a little disappointed he'd been
Chosen. I liked him as a friend, but he'd been shadowing
me for five years and often been a handful. I had hoped for
just a bit of time apart from him. That was not to be, it
seemed.

"This is Eona," he said introducing me to his Lumani,

with whom I'd not be able to speak. I nodded out of respect and said nothing.

You're not going to introduce us? Amya asked.

No, he's never going to be able to speak to you anyway.

You... don't like him?

I... my feelings for him are complicated.

Ah.

"Go ahead and grab a carriage," I said to him. I'll be along eventually.

"You're not coming?" he asked surprised. If there was one significant difference between the two of us it was that he was a rule-follower and I was a rule-breaker.

"No. I intend to stay here for the night and visit with my grandparents. I'll take the carriage in tomorrow. Silverveil isn't that far from here."

You're just going to throw off every tradition, aren't you?

Yup, are you sorry you Chose me yet?

Not yet.

"I..." I could see the conflict on Eadric's face. He'd so very much love to stay with me and meet my grandparents, but he also must have been told by Eona, that proceeding straight to Silverveil was the proper course of action. "I'll stay with you," he said firmly.

That was a surprise.

"Oh?" How far was he willing to go with this, I wondered. "Then send away your carriage. You won't need it. You can ride in mine tomorrow."

You're just being cruel now, Amya said, but there wasn't much reproach in his voice, just observation.

Yup.

"What about the names and information that are inside the carriage?" Eadric balked.

I knew how I was going to handle all of that, but I

wanted to see what he'd do without telling him. "Are you going or staying?" I asked.

"Staying!" he decided and marched over to a carriage and had a short fight with the driver before the driver shook his head and left. Eadric returned. "I'll go with you, tomorrow."

So, he *could* break the occasional rule, interesting. Perhaps I'd misjudged him.

Having spent the last five years with him, I'd gotten used to disregarding him, but I took a long look at him now. He was short for a human, but average height for a male Fey, and still several inches taller than me. His obsidian black hair was cropped short, but in a haphazard style which left some of his bangs hanging low, over one eye. His eyes were jewel-toned, like all Fey, a dark amethyst, intense and large. Fey didn't grow facial hair, so his face was smooth and fresh, with a small mouth and button nose. He was wiry, long lean muscles on his small frame, but far stronger than he looked. He was handsome enough. And he'd literally followed me around the world, so he was dedicated enough. The trouble wasn't with him... but with me. I just wasn't ready to settle down with one man yet, and I might never want just one man. So, I'd done everything to test his love... and still he remained with me.

I sighed. I'd have to talk to him soon about how I felt, but not now.

I spoke to my own driver and told him to find some place to stay for the night, I even provided him the coin to do so. He was surprised but obliged me. Then, I marched off toward my grandparents' house with Eadric in tow. "This way."

CHAPTER 3

ASHA / FEATHER

It would be a long trip to Silverveil. I'd have lots of time to read whatever was in the envelope which had been left in the carriage, but I'd snatched it up not long after we were under way and read it. My education had been... sporadic. I'd attended the small school in Bell Cove until I was twelve then been left to my own devices. There wasn't a school for those any older as most children began trades at that age. I, however, was not interested in becoming a seamstress like my sister and most of the other trades in the village had focused on fishing, which hadn't interested me at the time. So, I'd been a bit of a free spirit after that. Which meant I knew the basics of reading and writing and history, a bit of numbers, and not much more than that.

I opened the envelope and eagerly read the contents. There were three cards, the first said simply: Feather.

That will be your name when you get to Silverveil, Leoa said. *I think it's a beautiful name.*

The next card said: Bird.

You'll be a part of the Bird group. There will be others with names like yours, and you'll all study together working toward achieving a True-Bonding.

The last card said: Master Crab.

And it seems the instructor assigned to your group is named Crab. I haven't heard of him. I hope he isn't as his name suggests.

"Crabby?"

Exactly.

"Yes, let's hope." I leaned back on the soft cushions padding the bench of the carriage, enjoying the scenery rushing past the window. "I don't know what to expect at all, but I suspect you do. What can you tell me of... well everything I'll need to know?"

I felt Leoa's eagerness to spill everything to me as she hovered nearby, her pale pinks and blues mixing into shades of lavender and purple. *I can see working with you will be fun,* she began. I don't know why I thought of her as a "she," but her voice was definitely feminine, light and airy and free. *It's been so long since I've had a Chosen who knew nothing at all about Silverveil or Bonding.*

"Do most people know of these things?" I asked. I recalled mentions of them from my schooling, but I hadn't paid much attention in truth. I hadn't thought my life would go in this direction. I'd thought I'd be a loving wife and mother and that would be it. I'd been a wife, and though Davas and I had tried for kids, we'd not had any.

Leoa laughed. *Yes, many have dedicated their lives toward the single purpose of being Chosen. I sense that was not the case for you, and we'll have a long journey for you to tell me all about that. For now, let me tell you about what is to come.*

In several days we'll arrive at Silverveil. Once we're there, you will no longer be Asha, you'll be Feather.

I did find that name beautiful, but it didn't seem to fit me. I was not a light and slender "waif" of a girl. I had a woman's hips and heavy thighs. My waist may have been slender, but I had slightly squarish shoulders, strong arms, and a full bust. I had a body meant for childbearing, full and sturdy. The name "Feather" suggested a light and ephemeral woman, which I was not. Still, it was a lovely name, and I'd happily go by that until...

"Will Feather be my name from now on?"

I'd cut Leoa off as she'd progressed a bit, and she paused. *Ah... no, only while you are at Silverveil. When you are done at Silverveil one of two things will have happened. Either we will have come together as True-Bonded, and you'll get yet another name, or we will have not Bonded and you will return to being Asha.*

"Oh." I was a bit surprised by this. I had assumed that The Choosing had been all that was required for my new life. That there would be no returning to my old life. "That's an option? Not Bonding?"

It is, yes. It happens in about twenty percent of cases. I'm guessing Leoa sensed my confusion around the word "percent" and restated: *about one in five do not Bond. When that happens the Lumani returns to the Mists to await the next Choosing and the person returns to their old life. Generally, they cannot be Chosen again.*

"Oh." Now I was very curious and a little worried. "Why would we not Bond?"

Bonding isn't a choice. It just happens and no one — human or Lumani — know how or why. All we know is, some Bonds happen and others don't. The best guess we have is that it's a matching of spirits. When there is a match, the Bonding happens, and when there isn't, it doesn't.

"Do you think our spirits match?" I asked a bit tentatively. I didn't see a life for myself as Asha the widow of Bell Cove. I had hoped I'd be able to leave that behind.

I do. You are full of life and cheer, compassionate and caring, diligent and wise for your young age. And... I get the sense you have seen a lot of life for one so young and that is where your wisdom comes from. You've experienced loss and probably a greater range of emotions than most have at your age. That could pair well with any Lumani, but what truly calls to me is your overflowing love and your... sensuality.

"My... oh... truly?" It surprised me that a Lumani — a being of spirit and light — would be drawn to such things.

I assume you are sexually experienced. Am I wrong?

"No." She was definitely not wrong.

Let me guess, you have a big heart and lush body and men were drawn to you, yes?

I wouldn't have used those exact words, but... "Yes. I had a woman's body before I was thirteen. There was a boy, named Wilis, who had blossomed early as well." I don't know what compelled me to tell Leoa this, but if we were to Bond, I assumed we'd eventually know everything about each other anyway. "He'd been a beautiful young man: tall, though not yet filled into his frame, lean and lanky. "We... He was my first. We educated each other and became lovers and close friends. I might have remained with him... if his family hadn't arranged a marriage for him with a girl from Moon Harbor." I had been devastated that day. I'd thought we'd be together forever. He had felt the same way, and for a while we'd planned to run away. His family had urged him to at least meet the new girl. "Her name was Amantha. And when Wilis met her, there was a spark of something deeper than he and I had ever shared. Still, he hesitated. He even brought Amantha to meet me, telling her about us. And it was then that I knew... as intimate as Wilis and I had been, we were not meant for each other, not like he and Amantha were."

I'm so sorry, Feather. That is a hard thing to learn.

"It was, yes." I heard my voice become just a little lost and nostalgic. "But I still look back fondly on my time with him." I let out a bit of a laugh. "And I can remember how Amantha's eyes went wide when I took her aside and told her all the things Wilis liked... in bed. Spirits, how she blushed, still a virgin. I made sure Wilis knew to be easy on her." I sighed. "They were a lovely couple."

But you miss him?

A tear traced my cheek, just the one. "Yes." I wiped the wetness away. "After that I helped several other boys in the village become men, preparing them for the women they'd be with, but I never allowed myself to get too close emotionally. I wasn't truly heartbroken for Wilis, I know that now. I was missing our connection and afraid to have — and lose — that again. What we had was fun and playful and loving, but it wasn't true love."

That came later, yes?

"Yes." And my heart constricted with the still-too-recent loss of Davas.

Oh... wow, I felt that. You don't have to talk about it if you don't want.

"I'll tell you everything, eventually, just not now. Why don't you tell me more about Silverveil? I want to be prepared; I want to make sure we Bond."

As you wish, Feather.

She told me of the campus and the dorms, of the types of classes and work to expect to help bind us together. She told of the many different young men and women who would be there, from all walks of life, though probably mostly from families of Nobility or high standing. *You are one who likes crowds, lots of people around, yes?*

That was a challenging question but the quick answer was: "No."

Oh?

I drew in a long breath. "I like people and I like to be around them, but I prefer close relationships with a few, going deep and letting them truly feel my emotions as I feel theirs."

Ah... yes, I understand. Well, then I do not know how you will fare at Silverveil. There will be many people around and some of the young men and woman are encouraged to... make strong connections while they are there. So... you may not enjoy the crowds but may enjoy the connecting.

I nodded to that. It seemed a fair assessment.

If I recall the Bird group correctly, there usually isn't more than five members, all named for parts of a bird.

"That will be nice, a good-sized group." I smiled. I wasn't quite sure where my next words came from. "I also hope there is a young woman I can connect with."

Oh? Are you... attracted to women? Or perhaps you wish to explore that side of yourself?

"No, not really." I had only ever been attracted to men, though I saw the beauty in everyone. And as I thought about this more, I had my own little revelation: "I just... want a friend, a close friend, like Wilis was, but without the sex." I blinked a little. Having said it aloud, it sounded so simple. Yet, I'd never had anyone like that. I had known other young woman in the village and been close with my niece — who was more like a twin sister, we were born only a few months apart — but, I'd never had a true, close friend. Perhaps it was because I'd always confided in my mother and sister for those sorts of things. Now that I didn't have them around, I was realizing how much I'd missed that and wished for it.

I hope you find that too. Some of the girls may be more preoc-

cupied with finding a man, but you are kind and open and I'm sure someone will open up to you.

"That would be nice."

And, if a young man were to ask to kiss you, or... more?

"If he was handsome and didn't wish for any deep connection, I'd allow it." I was missing Davas, but I wasn't dead. If a man were up for some fun with no attachments, I might be willing to see how... experienced he was; maybe even to teach him a little.

No deep connection? But I thought that's what you wanted? Something must have occurred to Leoa then as her tone changed. Ah... yes, right, you are still feeling the loss of a true love and don't wish for anything like that yet, yes?

"Yes." But we were once again getting a bit too close to that subject. "What about Bonding? How does that happen?" I asked.

The instructors will tell you there is no one way to Bond, and that is true, but... what is also true is that all True-Bonds happen essentially the same way. You... share a connection through some dominant aspect of your spirit and your Lumani's. Yet that aspect varies dramatically from person to person and Lumani to Lumani, so... True-Bonds are formed in a great variety of ways.

"If you had to guess, what would be my dominant aspect, what might we Bond over?" I really wanted to expedite this process if possible.

Leoa laughed, a light and airy sound. We share several aspects in common, Feather. There is our... ah... lusty nature. There is how much we care for others. It could be how cheerful and vivacious we are. Or, it could be our dedicated approach to everything we pursue.

That was a lot of options.

Don't worry, Feather, I'm certain we will Bond. Just... enjoy yourself, be yourself and it will happen.

"Thank you, Leoa, I will."

Speaking of enjoying yourself, isn't this beautiful countryside?

I glanced out the window again. We were passing through a lovely river valley, with lush farms on low rolling hills undulating away from the wide, serene flow of the river. "It is."

You said you'd never been this far from your home before, yes?

"That's right. I've never been north of Peter's Town."

Then relax and enjoy the ride.

So, I did.

CHAPTER 4

DAWN

My grandparents were surprised to see me. They hadn't even known I was in town and hadn't seen me in five years. Yet, I hadn't changed much in that time and they recognized me instantly, welcoming me in.

The Clarks were aging now, in their mid-sixties, with gray hair and wrinkles, but warm hearts... and minds filled with knowledge. They still worked at the library, though only half-days now and were home when I arrived at their small dwelling.

They embraced me warmly, then Grandad asked who I'd brought with me. I introduced Eadric as a close friend and they smiled knowingly at each other. They thought we were more than friends, and I didn't dissuade them of that. My relationship with Eadric was too complicated to explain quickly or easily.

Eadric and I sat at the kitchen table as the two of them puttered around the hearth preparing a meal.

"You've been gone a long time," Grandad said. There was no rebuke in his tone, but a little concern. "Your mother was worried."

"Oh?" I said just a little surprised. I knew my parents cared about me, but they'd always been distant. Running two nations wasn't easy, and they'd had limited time to spend with me.

Grandad stopped what he was doing and looked at me. "Yes, Dawn. I know... she may have had trouble showing it at times, but she loves you. She and Alvere both. When you disappeared with nothing but that letter, they were... more than a little concerned."

I grimaced. "For the heir to Vauphan, not me."

Eadric raised his brow at me.

Do you truly believe your parents cared more that you were the heir to a nation, than for you as their daughter? Amya seemed a bit shocked. *I will admit, in my previous life, I was a captain in the Southern Navy and did not hear much about our illustrious Queen and King, but what I did hear was that they cared deeply for those around them and their nations.*

Oh, they cared. I spoke aloud to share my thoughts with everyone. "I know they cared about me, but they had a strange way of showing it. Once I was old enough to truly converse with them intelligently, they shipped me off to Ona Ahmaia and the Fey."

"I am thankful they did, or I would not have met you," Eadric said solemnly.

I wasn't so thankful. I'd learned a lot from the Fey and Ona Ahmaia, but... "I'd wanted to be with my parents. They could easily have had tutors teach me the ways of others. That way, I could stay with them." I sighed heavily. Both my grandparents had pity in their eyes. I hated that look. I wasn't to be pitied. I'd made the best of what I had.

"If you wanted to be with them so much, why did you run away when you were to have returned to them?" Granny asked.

"They were just going to ship me off somewhere else to learn more lessons, I'm sure."

Granny seemed to want to say something, but Grandad put a hand on her arm and shook his head. Instead, he looked at me with a soft smile. "Tell us about the places you visited."

I smiled back at him; now that was a topic I liked talking about.

I am curious as well. I have always loved to travel. As a captain in the navy, I saw many ports but not much more of foreign lands. Otherwise, I know only of Elista. Amya seemed to quiver with anticipation. The entire reason the Lumani Bonded with people was so they could experience as much of the world and the physical and emotional life of humans as they could.

I felt my own excitement pique as I stirred my memories. I had seen so many strange and wonderful things and places and peoples. "This is truly an amazing world, Grandad, and I have been blessed to see so many amazing things! It may have been wrong to run off, but I would do it all again in a heartbeat. After we left the North, we spent nearly a month at sea before we arrived in the nation of Isharu. It is a prosperous and peaceful nation where their spiritual leaders spend hours, sometimes days or even years in meditation with the gods of their lands. They say these Dhar'me actually speak to the gods, commune with them and petition on behalf of their people for peace and mild weather, good crops and bountiful harvests, and so on. I was able to visit one of their temples and despite the many people there, it was so quiet. I saw these men and women, fasting and meditating and in such a state of peace, it was amazing!" I couldn't help the giddy tone to my voice. I rarely got so excited about anything, but as more memories flooded back to me, I smiled with remembered wonder.

"We travelled on sand-ships across the shifting dunes of Zuvanyika, where the original dragons live beneath the sands. They're called... I can't remember the name in their language, but they're called Fire Wyrms, which is apt because it was blazing hot there. There were also people called Okuri who could breathe fire, said to be descended from dragons somehow! Isn't that wonderous!"

Eadric said nothing, his usual quiet self. But I could see the wonder in his eyes as he recalled our adventures. My grandparents were already wide-eyed. I wouldn't have expected that from two learned elders, but apparently there were a few things these two highly intelligent people didn't know.

More likely it's that you have experienced what they may only have read about.

Ah, yes, true. Reading about something and seeing it are vastly different.

Indeed.

"In the Helea lands there were lush valleys and high mountains. It's not so much a nation as it is a region, filled with many curiosities. There are a people there called the Necromila who commune and speak to the spirits of the dead, even animating the bones of their ancestors to do labor for them. Their army of the dead is fearsome to behold. Luckily it isn't that large an army." I felt a shiver run through me at the memory.

"And also in Helea, were the strangest of all the peoples we met, because they weren't even people! The Exypnozah —" I felt my tongue stumble over the word, and I'd practiced it a lot. "—are not human at all, they're intelligent animals of all sorts, who have their own society! Their mythology suggests that long ago, some nature spirit or god loved her creatures so much she gifted them with an awakening of their minds, and they have flourished ever since!" I couldn't help but smile at the gaping mouth of my grandad. "I know!"

Grandad turned to Granny. "We have read so much, scribed books our entire lives, why have we never heard of such amazing beings?"

Granny grinned. "There is only so much knowledge from outside of Elista that reaches us. Our library may be vast, but it is far from complete."

Grandad nodded. "Yes, of course."

"And I'm not done," I said seeing their excited looks.

Truly? There are more wonders? Amya asked, also sounding awed.

"Oh yes, from Helea we travelled across the Uru Mountains, a vast swath of jagged peaks, which would otherwise be impassable, except... there is a nation who live in this inhospitable region and they've found an amazing way to get from place to place. They have flying ships! From small balloon-boats to massive ships. They've found some gas, which they use to float these ships and you rise so high, the mountains simply slip by below you!"

"I think I've heard of them," Grandad said softly, still awed. "But I wasn't sure I believed it."

"It's true. They are a people without any great gods or spirits or magic, but they have developed machines powered by steam and gasses and built cities into the sides of mountains!"

"I did not much like flying," Eadric said, sounding a bit queasy. Indeed, he had been sick and miserable the entire trip. "Fey were not meant to be separated from the Great

Mother." The Fey revered the earth itself as the mother of their race and all living beings.

I patted him on the back, sympathetic for that horrible time for him. I'd found it thrilling and exciting. I wished he could have enjoyed it.

"From there we travelled to the Empire of Weijin. They have carved their nation from the earth and water itself. The Shuitujike seemed to do the impossible, singing songs that move earth and water. They use this power to build cities, irrigate farms, propel their ships, and even bring earth to life in the form of a man to carry amazing loads for them."

I couldn't help the grin on my face widening even more. The place I'd most enjoyed during my southern travels had been the last I'd visited, and I felt myself quiver with remembered joy. "The last place we visited was a nation where women rule and men are subservient laborers." I couldn't help a laugh. "I loved it. It was called Ayshia, home of the Uanitabankua people. They are a peaceful and intelligent nation, though they can battle fiercely when needed. They live in tune with nature and the spirits. They even speak to the spirits, asking them for boons and blessings. I could only dream to be as strong as some of those women, who were so lightning quick with sword and spear and bow that I couldn't imagine trying to face them. Indeed, the nation of Weijin to the south tried to expand in to Ayshia lands and were rebuffed again and again, despite larger armies and warriors of solid earth! They've given up now and are at peace with the Uanitabankua." I couldn't help the awe in my own voice, amazed at what that small, but powerful nation had accomplished.

"Are all their men laborers?" Grandad asked.

"Not all, no. I think there is a test they can take, and if they pass, they are allowed to become merchants and scholars and such, but they are never warriors. The men there are small and weak, where the women are tall and strong. It's fascinating!"

"And what did they think of you?" Granny asked.

I got the hint. I was small and slight, though far stronger than I looked, all traits of my Fey blood. I was only one-quarter Fey, but their blood ran strong within me.

"Once I'd proven my strength to them, they called me 'Pahlawa kecil.' It means tiny warrior. They were amazed that one as small as I could be so strong." I turned to Eadric. "And they called Eadric: 'Leki Logam,' which means metal man, since he could bend metal to his will."

Eadric was smiling. He'd been just a little proud of the fact that these strong tall women had been amazed by what he — a small, slight man — could do.

I sighed heavily, still smiling, my memories filling me with a warm nostalgia. "It was an amazing time." Another heavy sigh. "And now I'm home."

And a new adventure awaits you, Amya said with certainty.

Oh, how are you so sure?

Because... I know me and I know you. Together... we'll make our own adventure. I can't wait.

And suddenly... neither could I.

CHAPTER 5

DAWN

T<small>HE NEXT DAY</small> I <small>WAS EAGER TO BE OFF TO</small> S<small>ILVERVEIL</small>.

Eadric and I found our carriage and climbed in.

"You take the envelope," I said hiking my legs up to cross them under me on the cushioned bench. My feet couldn't touch the floor and I hated having them dangle. "I'm not changing my name, nor do I care about any of the rest."

"Truly?"

He's been with you for how long now and still doesn't really understand you, does he? Amya asked.

No, though... I'm not sure I understand him either. As I said before we have a complicated relationship.

Eadric opened the envelope and read aloud from the cards within. "My new name will be Quartz. I'm in the Stone group, led by... Lady Rhea." He looked up at me. "I'm sure if you wanted to join my group, they'd let you. I could—"

"No, Eadric or Quartz or whatever... Just... no." I sighed. The time had come. "We need to talk and being stuck in a carriage together seems the perfect time to do it."

His pale brow was furrowed, amethyst eyes just a little

hurt. I don't know why he looked like that, all puppy-dog wounded. He should have known this was coming.

"Eadric, I... I appreciated you coming with me on my journeys these past few years. As much as I hate to admit it, I was lonely from time to time, and having a friend around was nice." That was the kindest way I could put it. There had been some days when having a friend around — someone who spoke my language — had been truly a blessing.

I saw his soft smile. Now came the hard part; hard for him, not for me. "And I think now is a good time for us to start to find out who we are on our own."

More frowns and furrows.

"We won't be that far apart, both at the same place, just in different dorms. I think that will be good for us. It's not that I don't like you, or want to be away from you, but... you've been with me for so long now, I need... some space. I want to get to know more people, make more friends. So... no, I don't want to be in your group. I'll find another group to attach myself to. I hope you understand."

His jaw was tense, lips tight, and I thought him on the verge of tears. For a Fey he was very emotional. But then he swallowed hard and nodded. "If that is what you want."

"It is, yes. Thank you for understanding."

He looked away out the window at the passing country-side for a long time and I thought the conversation over.

I was wrong.

"How do you feel about me?" he asked after perhaps nearly an hour of silence.

Ah... and there it was. It had only taken him following me around the world and back to finally ask.

I could be blunt or diplomatic. I'd try diplomatic first. "You're a dear friend, Eadric, and I know you would like to be more, but... you're a little too... intense." How to say this? "You don't build a fire by smothering it with wood, you build a fire by giving it the small bits it needs and letting it breathe." He hadn't looked at me, but I saw his face turn tight again, expression hard. "Do you understand?"

"I do," he said just a little too quickly. "Somehow, me being there for you — being everything you needed — these past five years has smothered you? Is that it? I never once spoke of love, I only tried to be the best companion I could be!"

It was time to be blunt. "I don't love you, Eadric. I don't know if I'll love anyone, ever. Maybe love isn't for me. I'm all for sex, some physical fun, but I knew you'd think it more than just that and I didn't want to hurt you. I do like you, as a friend, and have appreciated you being there, but I know you want more and I just... don't." I'd finally said it.

Pain lanced through Eadric's eyes, and he turned away, tears on his cheeks.

It was my turn to look out at the passing countryside. Suddenly it felt very close and cramped in this carriage.

"You think you know, but you don't." Eadric's voice was harsher than I'd ever heard it; acidic. "Do you want to know how I really feel about you?"

I sighed. I was fairly certain I already knew, but we might as well get it all out now. "How do you feel?"

"I've loved you since the moment I saw you, Dawn. You're... so... infuriatingly beautiful and amazing. Your blush is... intoxicating." His voice was growing heated, heavy.

None of this was news to me. His mention of my "blush" made me grimace and shake my head.

Why? Do you not blush? Amya asked, curious.

For a human, I am extremely pale. Some have said I have

skin like alabaster. But for a Fey, I am... exotic. They are as fair skinned as I am, but when I get excited, apparently, I have a blush which turns my cheeks a subtle pink, which for the Fey is an extremity of color upon the skin. My Ona told me it would probably drive most Fey men crazy with desire. I had hoped she was joking. She wasn't.

Oh? That is fascinating.

Not for me.

Ah.

Eadric was going on... and on... "You are truly like the dawn for which you are named, a thankful and refreshing brightness, lifting the world from the depths of darkness. You are the pale new light of day and full of so much heat and energy, so much purpose and drive. No Fey has ever been to see the world as I have. They have no desire to leave their home and the connection to the earth they feel there. But you... you feel that same connection, I know you do, but still had to explore everything else. How could I not follow you? How could I resist the intensity of your lure? My heart cries out every hour of every day to be with you and I had to be at your side. And I don't regret a moment of it, not even the flying ships." That was a bit of a surprise. I was certain he'd hated that. "Dawn, I love you with every fiber of my being, and I will always love you."

I looked at him then. He'd turned from his window. Fey didn't blush — like I did — when they were feeling heated and excited, but instead, their eyes seemed to nearly glow, luminous with intensity. And Eadric's eyes were glimmering pools of amethyst, so raw and full of energy I was entranced for just a moment. I'd known he loved me, but never the true depths of his affections.

He did follow you around the world and back.

True...

"Always," Eadric repeated softly and the light began to fade from his eyes. He turned away then, to look back out the window. "So, if you ever change your mind; if your heart ever thaws enough to desire a true companion, I will be there. You just need to call." He sighed heavily. "And for now, I will do as you ask and give you space. I will only ever do as you wish, and if this *is* what you wish, I will obey."

"It is."

He nodded curtly.

Wow. I blinked a bit, turning away just in case he might see the single tear in my eye. I reached up to "scratch my cheek" and wipe it away.

That was heartfelt. I have known a love like that, Amya said softly.

Have you? And did the one you love break your heart by refusing you?

No, we both knew we were meant for each other.

My mother has four lovers. Her husband, plus two other men and a woman. She says she feels the same intensity of love for all of them. I... have never felt like that for anyone.

Amya sighed. *I hope you do, young one, I hope you do. It is a sad and empty life if you've never experienced such abiding love.*

And what if they break my heart? I asked, my soul trembling. I'd loved my parents and they'd never been there, never loved me as I'd loved them. I still hated them for it.

That is the risk you take with emotions as intense as these. But there are some who say that it is better to have felt that intensity of love, and the corresponding intensity of loss, than never to have felt it at all.

I wasn't sure I believed that. I was all for sex, keeping things physical and fun, even though I was fairly inexperienced in that area. My only encounter with a man had been when we'd been in the South. Eadric and I had visited a

pleasure palace in Weijin. Eadric had been dubious —
which I now understood a little better — but I'd been curious. We had each ordered a man and a woman to our rooms
to explore what we desired. A Shuitujike had sung softly —
from behind a rice-paper wall — to the waters within us,
stirring our blood to passion. I found my time with the
woman curious and very enlightening, but I decided that
was not truly what I desired. But the man had been strong
and forceful, while also being soft and caring in his ministrations. And when I'd felt the fullness of him inside me, I'd
known I wanted more of that. I had no qualms about the
purely physical kind of love. When it came to my emotions,
however, I was much more guarded. I would not let anyone
hurt me — the way my parents had — again.

You will live a very lonely life if you never open up to anyone,
Amya said softly, tenderly. *I know your parents were distant,
but that doesn't mean everyone will be. You may need to risk
getting close to someone... eventually.*

Perhaps, was all I'd give him. I wouldn't exclude the
possibility entirely, but I sure as The Black Pits wasn't going
to go seeking it out. As far as I was concerned, emotional
love only led to pain.

All I had to do was look at Eadric to understand it. If
someone did to me what I'd just done to him, I'd never want
to risk loving ever again.

So why risk it in the first place?

*Sometimes the heart chooses for you and you have little say
in the matter, as was probably the case for poor Eadric.*

My heart will do exactly as I tell it to do.

Amya sighed and I got the distinct impression of him
shaking his head, but he said no more, which was good. I
was done with talk of love.

My mood had not improved by the time we reached

Silverveil. The trip from Miraline to Silverveil usually took about four hours by regular coach. Those who had been Chosen yesterday had arrived late in the afternoon. We'd left mid-morning and arrived at Silverveil early that afternoon.

Eadric was out quickly and marching toward the male instructor awaiting him.

I got out slowly, taking in the large compound. It was functional, not much in the way of flair in the design or layout. Squat squared buildings and a roughly symmetrical design, there wasn't much to see really.

I grabbed my heavy travel pack and approached the female instructor.

"Name?" she asked.

"Dawn." I smiled, knowing she wouldn't find it on her lists.

"No, the name from your card. While you are at Silverveil you will—"

"No, I won't," I cut in quickly. "I'm not changing my name and you can either assign me a room or I'll take one. As you can see, I've got a Lumani with me. I've been Chosen, so let's get this over with, shall we?"

The woman wore a look of shocked indignation. "I have never—"

"Are you going to give me a room number or not?"

"I most certainly will not! You—"

"I am Princess Dawn, daughter of Queen Legs of House Spider and daughter of Alvere of Vauphan, princess-heir to the throne of Vauphan. And because I'm heir to the throne of Vauphan, I can't go around changing my name all the time, so accept it and give me a room!" I hated having to do that, and I hated this woman for making me do it. I didn't like my titles and didn't want to be heir to anything.

The woman snapped her gaping mouth shut. "Oh..." She looked — dazed and dumbfounded — at me for a long moment, then looked down at her list. "You can have room twelve in the primary dorm, just over there." She made a note.

"Thank you," I said, probably more harshly than I had to, and marched off to my room.

Oh, you're going to be so much trouble... and so much fun, Amya said, laughing.

Yes, I would.

I got to my room and immediately disliked it. It was on the north side of the building. I would have much preferred one on the south side. So, I checked the doors along the southside until I came to room seventeen, which was open. This had been my mother's room. As much as I wanted a room facing south, I didn't want *this* one, but it was my only choice.

Well Pits.

That only made my mood worse, but I took room seventeen.

And now you're changing rooms without telling anyone. You're going to drive people crazy, you know that, right?

It'll be a small perk.

Amya laughed again.

I flopped down on the bed. I didn't much care if I missed supper, I was tired and emotionally exhausted and just wanted to rest.

Amya settled on the pillow near my head, and I felt a soothing warmth filter through me.

Rest, he said softly.

And I did.

CHAPTER 6

ASHA / FEATHER

I ARRIVED AT SILVERVEIL FIRST THING IN THE MORNING, MY carriage actually had to wait until the gates were opened. There were three other carriages waiting as well, lined up behind us. From what I'd learned from Leoa, we were getting close to the end of the arrival period. These four carriages were probably the last. I should have arrived the previous day, but a broken wheel had delayed us by a half a day.

When the gates finally opened, I could barely contain myself. I had the carriage door half open as we drove in, peering wide-eyed at my new home, at least for the next few weeks. I was even more certain now that Leoa and I would Bond soon. Already our connection had deepened and we'd chosen our avatar form. She had transformed from a ball of swirling pink and blue to a small rodent of the same mixed colors. I couldn't identify the small animal, but it was — in my opinion — incredibly cute. It had two long back legs and two barely-there, front legs. It seemed to hop more than run. It also had a long tail, which ended in a tuft of fur. Currently, Leoa, in mousy form, sat on my shoulder, looking around with eyes, which — she'd told me — couldn't really see. As much as she looked like an animal, she wasn't. She was still a ball of energy and had other ways of sensing the world. She wouldn't be able to see until we Bonded and she became a part of me.

I hopped from the carriage even before it had fully stopped and hurried to the woman with sheafs of paper.

"I'm Feather, who are you?" I asked excitedly.

The woman blinked, seemingly a little surprised at my question. "I am Lady Angora." She looked at her papers. "And yes, here you are, the last of the young ladies we're expecting. You've been assigned room seventeen in the primary dorm, just over there. "She indicated with her pencil. "Welcome to Silverveil."

"Thank you!" I said, eager to see my room. I tried not to run, it wouldn't be lady-like — that woman had referred to me as a young lady after all — but couldn't help myself and bounded over to the dorm.

Once inside, I searched down the hall and came to room seventeen on the left. But upon opening the door I found a girl sleeping on my bed.

"Ah... hello?" I said, a bit confused. I checked the number on the door again. Yes, it was the right room. "I think this is my room?"

The girl stirred and opened her eyes, sitting up slowly.

I immediately reassessed her. I'd thought her a girl because she was small, but as she roused and I saw her a bit clearer, it was evident she was a young woman like me. Moreover, even with her hair disheveled from sleep, she was gorgeous! She had skin like alabaster, so pale and pristine, a stark contrast to her short-cut raven-black hair. Her eyes were a nearly luminescent sunshine gold in hue, like two brilliant gems. She had a diamond-shaped face with the faintest brush of color on her full cheeks. She was slight of build with slender arms and legs, but still with the bloom of womanhood upon her.

Every so often, I wished I were more girlish in my look, but mostly I loved my full figure and how it made men drool.

"Who are you?" she asked groggily.

"I'm Asha!" I said quickly, before remembering... "No, I'm Feather now. Who are you?"

"Dawn."

"That's a lovely name." Now that that was over, I got back to my main point. "I think there's been a mix-up, I was told this was to be my room?"

"Yeah, I stole it. I wanted the southern exposure and it was the only one left on this side of the building. Sorry. You can have my room, it's twelve."

I blinked, then shrugged. I didn't really care which room I had, nor did I care if it faced south or north. I'd probably prefer north actually. It would get less light in general and if it was to be mainly where I slept, what did I care about light? However...

"Won't the instructors be confused? Do they need to know our rooms?"

No, not really, they don't come to get you in the dorms most days, unless you're horribly late for lessons, so switching shouldn't be a problem.

Oh, thank you! I was slowly getting the feel for speaking to Leoa in my head.

"They don't care," Dawn said, stretching. She reminded me of a cat, lithe and small.

"Oh... then I'll gladly take your room. I don't much care for sun one way or the other."

"Good, thanks," she said and rose. There was a part of

me which envied her easy grace of movement. Also, she was even smaller than I'd thought, barely five feet. I was a full head taller than her. Yet, there was some sort of aura of power around her. Even though she was small, I felt if she told me what to do, I'd do it.

"Is something wrong?" she asked, and I realized I'd been staring at her.

"If I might say so, you are gorgeous and graceful and somehow powerful." I'd never been one to temper my words. I said what I felt.

Dawn's eyes went wide. "Ah... thanks? But I'm not into women."

"Oh, neither am I, except as friends."

"But you..." She blinked. Her brow furrowed. "So, you just felt like telling me I'm gorgeous?"

I smiled. "I like to compliment people whenever I can." I shrugged. It was just me, I liked to make people feel good about themselves and I was usually able to find something positive to say. In Dawn's case it was easy.

She smiled, head tilting to one side. "In that case. I think you're the gorgeous one, I'd kill for your curves... and your height."

I smoothed my dress over my too-large hips and heavy thighs. "You're very kind to say so, thank you."

She shook her head and sighed. "Sorry, I was half asleep when you introduced yourself, what was your name again?"

"Feather."

"It has been a thorough pleasure to meet you, Feather." Dawn smiled. "I didn't expect the girls I'd meet here to be so kind and generous of spirit. I figured they'd mostly be Nobles' brats. You are a breath of fresh air." She approached and put a hand on the door. "Now if you'll excuse me, I think I want a shower before breakfast."

Leoa had told me about the showers, and given my long journey, that seemed like a great idea.

"Oh! Do you mind if I join you?"

She quirked a dark brow.

"Not in the same shower," I amended quickly. "I've just never seen these showers before and I just got in from a long carriage ride and—"

Dawn laughed, a light and full sound. "Yeah, sure, Feather, but you'll want to grab your dress from your room. There should be one that fits you." She laughed. "Unless you're like me and can't stand the sight of them and insist on wearing your own clothes."

"Oh, can we do that? I didn't bring anything with me. I was told everything would be provided."

"*Can* we do it? Sure. Do they *like* it? No. But I don't care. Now hurry up and get your clothes." She shooed me out of her room and I hurried back down the hall to room twelve. There were indeed three dresses laid out on the bed. The mid-sized one looked like it would be tight on me, so I plucked up the largest one and hurried back to Dawn, who was leaving her room with what looked like a man's shirt and pants hung over her arm.

"This way," she said and led me down the hall to an alcove off one-side. That led to a stairwell down, and then into the room with the baths and showers. It was already steamy down here. I guessed a few other girls had already bathed this morning.

"These are the showers," Dawn said, proceeding past the open landing area to where stalls were lined up side-by-side, along both sides of the room. She slipped into one, and I found an open door and went inside.

Leoa guided me through the different elements: hooks to hang my clothes — both the set I'd brought and my old ones — and racks with towels. Then there was the inner tiled area with the knobs and soaps and the hot streaming water.

Once I got the water temperature right, I found the sensation amazing and marveled at the wonders of this place. I quickly washed myself, then luxuriated just a little in the warm waters, before stepping out and drying off.

As luck would have it, Dawn came out of her shower at the same time I did.

She looked over at me. "Oh... wow... ah... Sorry, but that dress does nothing for you."

Yeah, I had that feeling. It was very loose, which was good, because I was on the larger side, when it came to hips and chest. The trouble was, even though there was a belt I could use to show off my hourglass figure, the dress still felt like a bag on me. Dawn, however, looked amazing in tight black pants, showing off her slender legs, and a similarly tight silvery shirt, to emphasize her slight figure and slim arms. She had it buttoned up to her bust, but not above. It fell open revealing the tops of her small breasts and the expanse of perfect pale skin up to her delicate neckline.

"You, however, look great," I said.

"I know," she said with a grin. "But this is pretty much the only look that works for me. I don't tend to fill out most dresses the way they were intended."

I smiled as we made our way back up to our rooms. "I have a little skill with a needle, I could try to make you something that shows off what you have," I offered.

Dawn gave a breathy chuckle. "Don't worry yourself. There will be a seamstress coming tomorrow. I'll get her to do it. She won't want to, but I have ways of convincing people to do what I want."

"I bet you do... you're so... confident and commanding."

She gave another laugh, this one sounding a bit more derisive. "Yes, and everyone loves a domineering woman."

I shrugged. "Some people do." I wasn't sure about women, but I'd had experiences with many types of men. Some were strong and sure and in charge, and others liked to defer to women. "Just be you and people will love you, I'm sure." Though I'd had to do more than just be myself to catch Davas. He'd not been interested at first, but I'd worked hard to—

I cut those thoughts off, quickly. Only pain remained if I followed those initially warm and loving memories all the way to the end.

"I like you, Feather. What group are you in?" Dawn asked.

I was fast growing fond of this beautiful, confident woman, and it would be wonderful if we happened to be in the same group.

What do you think Leoa, isn't she fascinating and beautiful?

I have to admit, I sense something about her... or perhaps her Lumani, which I also find appealing, Leoa said. *I am very curious to find out more about her. I do hope she is in your group and you get a chance to get to know each other.*

Perhaps, even if she isn't, we'll get to spend some time together.

Perhaps, but the days are long here, spent mostly with your group, and you'll probably be tired at the end of most days. You may not see her as much if she's in another group.

Oh.

"I'm in the Bird group. Is that your group?" I asked hoping it would be.

Dawn was suddenly grinning ear to ear. "It is now."

CHAPTER 7

DAWN

I LIKED FEATHER. SHE WAS SO FULL OF LIFE AND CHEER, A breath of fresh air. As much as I'd been hoping to make new friends at Silverveil, I hadn't expected them to just walk into my room. Still, she was so ebullient and vivacious I couldn't help but smile around her. So, I decided that I'd join her group.

We went to the great hall to get our breakfast, and I was happy to note the number of surprised looks I got.

I didn't think you liked attention? Amya asked, curious.

That was true. *Most of the time, yes, but today I want to make sure I stand out. If I'm to meet some new people here, then I need to be someone others remember.*

From what I heard, your mother stood out on her first day, wearing a dress two sizes too small and showing off her namesake legs.

Yeah, don't remind me. I haven't heard that story a thousand times.

Ah, right, understood, shutting up about your mother.
Much appreciated.

"This is so exciting!" Feather was practically bubbling

with energy. I couldn't help but smile. "And everyone's looking at you. See, didn't I tell you you're beautiful!"

"Put the right clothes on you and they'd all be looking at you instead." Of that I was certain. My companion, though her current outfit did nothing to show off her figure, was amazingly proportioned. She had all the womanly curves I had longed for since I'd come of age. I was straight with small breasts, though this shirt did do a lot with what little cleavage I had. But Feather was all woman, heavy bust and full hips with that narrow waist, it gave her a nearly perfect hourglass figure. Then there was the smooth, tawny skin of her round face, dark pools for eyes, and all perfectly framed by a wavy fall of auburn hair.

"The pair of us will steal all the men, won't we?" she whispered to me, conspiratorially.

I laughed. That wasn't what I'd come here to do, but... sure. "I'm not really up for a relationship now, but I wouldn't mind a fun encounter or two with a handsome man."

"Oh... wow, me too. I ah..." I sensed the temporary dip in her otherwise jovial mood, but it was gone in a moment. "I just got out of a long-term thing and mostly want something fun and meaningless."

"Then it's decided," I said with mock seriousness. "We'll find ourselves some boy-toys, make them pleasure us until we've had our fill, then toss them away."

Feather laughed. "I'm not sure I'd put it that way, but... yeah, sure."

We ate together, sitting a bit apart from the rest of the Chosen, so we could talk privately. Feather said there wasn't much of interest in her past, but the more I heard, the more I found her story fascinating:

"My mother died giving birth to me." She didn't seem to have much emotion around this, but perhaps that made sense, if you never knew a person it would be difficult to mourn them. "So, I was raised by my sister, who was much older and already had a child of her own. For the longest time I thought she was my mother. She took care of me like I was her own child and my niece and I were raised as sisters." I listened intently, captivated. "When I was old enough, my mother told me she was actually my sister and explained what had happened. But I continued to think of her as my mother and my niece as my sister, that just seemed natural."

I shook my head.

Have you ever heard of such a thing? I asked Amya.

Yes, it's not common, but it happens, though usually the older sibling isn't old enough to have children of their own at the same time.

"I grew up in a fishing village and was given pretty much free rein to do as I pleased. My duties were light. I had to attend school, which was a half day, then I helped around the house a little. But mostly my sister and I ran free, building palaces of sand on the beaches or running into the waves to swim in the sea. We sometimes dug for crabs and mussels to bring home for dinner."

"Spirits," I breathed. "That sounds wonderful!" So free and wild in an idyllic sea-side setting.

Feather smiled softly, full lips spreading wide. "It was," she said with a heavy sigh of nostalgia. "Then... I became a woman and everything changed."

"Oh?" I could imagine that must have been a significant change for her, but I was curious how exactly.

"I developed early, and one day when my sister and I came out of the waters from swimming naked, I noticed a group of boys, wide-eyed and giggling as they watched us. I didn't understand at first, but my mother told me that I'd not be able to swim naked so... freely from then on. By thirteen I was mostly as you see me now, but my thighs and hips hadn't filled out so much."

"Thirteen?" I felt envious and sorry for Feather all at once. That was a young age to be a full-bodied woman. I was twenty and I still wasn't a full-bodied woman.

"Oh, yes. By then I was getting a lot of looks from young men. It was an awkward time..." She sighed and smiled. "Then I met Wilis."

"Oh? And had he matured early too?"

Feather giggled. "Well yes, but he was also a couple years older. He'd been working on his father's fishing boat for several years and his muscles were tight and long and lean. He was beautiful and all the girls were envious of me."

"And I'm sure all the boys were envious of him."

She smiled as if that hadn't occurred to her initially. "Yes, you're probably right."

"I know I am."

She smiled. "Anyway, soon I was running off far down the beach to go swimming with him instead of my sister."

"Naked?"

She giggled. "Of course."

"And was all of him as... long and strong as you described him?"

Feather giggled again. "Oh yes." Then she laughed outright. "Though our first time was so awkward and messy and uncomfortable, for both of us."

"How old were you?" I asked, a bit shocked and curious.

"I was fourteen by then, he was sixteen."

Spirits! My first time — that fancy brothel in Weijin — hadn't been until I was nineteen. This young woman was probably far more experienced than I was. "And was he the 'long term' thing you just got out of?" I asked, though regretted it as soon as I did, as Feather's face fell and she looked away.

"No." She shook her head. It took her a long moment, with deep breaths to regain herself. Yet, she was smiling when she turned back to me. "No, Wilis was amazing, but we were only together for about a year. His parents had arranged a marriage with a boat-builder's daughter from the next town over. We parted amicably and remained friends, though I didn't see him often as he went to live with his new bride."

"Oh, that sounds tough."

"It was... but ... there were other young men, who were interested."

"I'll bet there were."

She nodded, but her mood hadn't completely recovered and she seemed to fall back into a dark place when she said. "There was another man I loved. But... I'll tell you about him later, if that's well with you."

I nodded. "Of course." Whatever had happened with this other man, it must have ended badly. "You don't have to tell me at all if you don't want to."

She smiled softly at that. "Thank you, I... I think I do need to tell someone, eventually, but it's still a little fresh."

I nodded, taking the pressure off her. "Well, my story may have a few more chapters to it, but it still sounds like you've lived a full and rich life so far." I laid a hand on her shoulder, noticing my pale skin and small hand on her larger frame. We were so very different, the two of us, and yet, I felt we were on our way to becoming fast friends.

I told her a bit about my travels, skipping over my younger life and parentage. I also had things I didn't like people to know right away. And though we were interrupted by the summons to our groups, I was flattered by the wide-eyed amazement Feather showed at even just the first part of my foreign adventures.

Then... we met our group.

Our instructor, Master Crab, was a small man, aged and shriveled a bit, lost in his wrinkles. He had squinting, beady eyes — he probably required spectacles, but refused to use them — and a mouth with thin lips that protruded out, a little like a fish. As I had expected, he was very confused when he did his first count.

"Ah... I should have five of you," he said looking around. He blinked several times when he caught sight of me. "And I think you're out of uniform."

"I'm not wearing a uniform," I said evenly.

"I believe that's what I said." He grumbled a little. "You can change after we've done the roll call."

"No, I won't be changing, I'm not going to wear a uniform."

"Oh? Does the fabric give you a rash?" he nodded to himself without me answering. "Well tell the seamstress when she's working on you, and she'll arrange for something else."

I didn't acknowledge this.

He moved on. "Now, I believe one of you are in the wrong group, So, let's go through the list, shall we? Feather?"

Feather stood a little straighter. "Yes."

Crab looked at her for a long time, probably trying to get a rough sense for her vague shape and size so he'd remember her if he 'saw' her again with those aging eyes of his. "Good. Wing?"

"That's me!" a young man said. He was not that much taller than me, which would be exceptionally short for a man. He was thin and scrappy looking with a ready grin, dancing hazel eyes, and a spiky mop of brown hair. He winked at me when my gaze passed over him. He wasn't really my type; I'd spent the last few years with small and wiry and was hoping for a bit more of a man.

"Good, good," Crab muttered, gazing at Wing for a long moment. Then: "Plume?"

"Present." The polite and slightly haughty reply came from a pristine young woman. She was groomed to within an inch of her life, with not a single blond hair out of place, cosmetics upon her skin to shadow the lids over her bright blue eyes and accentuate the other features of her long face. She was clearly a Noble's daughter; from high society. Exactly the type I disliked and had wanted to get away from. She caught my glance and glared at me. She probably didn't like rule-breakers. I didn't care.

Crab peered at her for a long moment. "Yes, yes, all in order so far. Beak!" he called out and the tall young woman next to Plume started.

"Yes, ah, here, sir," the girl said. It was clear that she was not yet accustomed to her tall, lanky body, probably having recently had a growth spurt. She was awkward and seemed to sway on her long legs, while her gangly arms moved to keep herself balanced. She had a plain face with brown hair and eyes. Poor girl, she'd clearly stand out because of her height, but probably not much else.

"Very well, good, and last is Tail!" Crab called.

And my gaze moved to the scrumptious buffet of a man across the rough circle from me. Now *this* was someone I wanted to meet. He wasn't tall for a man, perhaps just a touch above average for his age, but it was clear he was very fit. His uniform was tight across a broad chest and thick arms but fell loose over his middle. His thighs were strong and straining against the fabric of his pants as well. He had the most delicious dark skin, a few shades darker than

Feather's, with an easy smile on his wide mouth, and intense dark eyes.

"That's right!" he said with an easy grin, turning a little to slap his own ass. "I'm Tail."

Hot and playful. Spirits! I could just eat him up!

"Oh!" Feather said. And given her tone, she agreed with my assessment. And it was clear she'd caught his eye as well as he winked at her. They'd be a near perfect couple; he was just a tad taller than she was and certainly all man. But I was just a bit jealous, I wanted him too.

But then that intense, dark gaze of his fell to me and he kept grinning. I felt my insides turn to liquid and heat rush to my core. Oh... he was going to be dangerous to be sure.

"He's handsome," Feather whispered, beside me.

"Oh, Pits, yes."

"Can we share him?"

I wouldn't mind that at all. "I get the feeling he wouldn't mind that."

"Good."

"And who didn't I call?" Crab cut into my reverie.

"Me," I said. "I'm not on your list, but I'll be joining this group. My name is Dawn."

"Down?" He blinked checking his list. "I didn't think we had a Down this year."

"No, Dawn," I insisted.

"Let him think what he likes," Feather whispered. And I nodded. Fair enough, as long as he accepted me into this group.

"That's what I said, Down." He sighed. "Someone messed up the lists again. I'll fix it."

I got the sense his hearing was just as bad as his eyesight.

The rest of the morning was spent going over the rules

and regulations and the process of what would happen over the next few weeks. I didn't pay much attention.

You don't think you'll need any of this to Bond with me? Amya asked.

I breathed a faint laugh, but mostly it was internal. *You Chose me because I was radical, so why would you think we'd Bond doing things the normal way?*

Fair point. Any thoughts on how you'd like to be radical?

I was mostly going to ignore what any instructor here told me and do my own thing. I gave a mental shrug. *Seems like the way to go if I want to be different.*

Understood. Ignore the rules and follow your own path. Got it.

Exactly.

So, I started immediately. When we were asked to pair up to try an exercise, I, instead, made a group of three, with myself, Feather, and Tail. He was happy. Plume wasn't. She'd been trying to snag him, and by the time she realized Master Crab was lost in his own world and wasn't going to break up our little group, Wing and Beak had already teamed up, which left her on her own.

And instead of practicing the movement exercise Crab had laid out, I pulled Tail aside and whispered to him. "My friend and I both think you're quite hot and were wondering if you'd like to sneak into our dorm tonight."

His easy grin widened. "You both want me? Together?" I could see the fantasy playing out behind his eyes.

"Not together," Feather clarified. "Separate, but we both want a turn."

He raised a brow at that.

"If only you had a twin," I said with a laugh.

"Ah... actually... I do," he said, matching my laugh.

"Don't kid with us. That would be too good to be true."

"I'm serious. His name is Agate. He's in the Stone group."

"He's here?"

Tail nodded.

Feather and I looked at each other for a long moment, sharing a naughty thought. "Then by all means, bring him tonight as well."

Tail's face fell just a little, but then his brow rose again as he asked. "If I bring him, would I still get to be with both of you? Could we switch out?"

So, I'd get to be with two matching, gorgeous young men in one night? Oh my.

I looked at Feather again. Her silly grin seemed to say: *would that just be too much?*

Why yes, it would, but if that's what he wanted, then, "Sure."

He grinned. "Wow, I saw you two and thought to myself, how will I ever choose between them! Now, I don't have to. Best day ever!"

I had to agree.

CHAPTER 8

FEATHER

I HEARD THE SOFT KNOCK ON MY DOOR. INSTANTLY, MY BODY responded with a thrill of heightened anticipation, blossoming from the low-level expectancy I'd been feeling all evening, waiting for Tail — or Agate — to arrive. I felt my heart pounding so hard my body seemed to vibrate. I rose and smoothed down my horrid-looking dress in an attempt to somehow make it look better, as a heady warmth set in, low in my stomach.

I went to the door, hand on the latch.

This is it! I said to Leoa who's small mouse-like form was perched on my desk. We had yet to determine what animal she was exactly.

Don't wait on my account, let him in. I'm curious.

Can you feel what I feel, even though we're not connected yet?

When your emotions are this strong, yes.

Something tells me you're going to feel all of what comes next, then.

Indeed. She seemed almost giddy with anticipation herself.

I opened the door and let in the beautiful, dark-skinned man, checking the hall and closing the door quickly behind him. As much as what we were doing was mostly expected at Silverveil, it was still officially against the rules for a boy to be in the girls' dorm.

"Are you Tail or Agate?" I asked, leaning against the door, just watching the young man swagger into my room. He exuded a certain sexy confidence. He knew he was hot and knew how to use that.

"It's me, Tail," he said, turning back to look me over ... and what a look it was. Lots of men gave me a once-over, but this was different. He unashamedly ran that dark-eyed gaze slowly up from my bare feet. And the way his eyes seemed to hungrily devour me, the slight lick of his lips as he passed my hips, the hot breath of wonder he let out when he paused at my chest, made that blossoming heat inside me explode into a bubbling lake of lava. I was sure I was blushing by the time he got to my face and other parts of me were even hotter still.

"My brother and I tossed a coin to see who would be with whom first. And I was lucky enough to get you first." He grinned and stepped in toward me, hands coming up to either side of my head, pressed to the door behind me, as he leaned in. His face was close, our noses brushing as he asked. "How do you want this to go? Are we flirting, making out, or more? All honesty, I'm not looking for a soulmate right now, but a little fun love works for me."

I smelled the fresh scent of the soaps from the bathing area upon him. He'd washed before he'd come. The slightly floral scent did nothing to take away from the masculine presence washing over me.

I put a hand on his chest, feeling the ridges of hard muscle under his shirt. I had to press my legs together to keep my heated core contained. He may have been young, but his body was all man. I swallowed hard, my voice husky and low as I said, "Fun love sounds good to me. I'm also not looking for anything lasting. As for the rest..." Looking into those dark eyes, I sensed Tail knew what he was doing, but just in case, I wanted to let him know to take it easy. "Why don't we take it slow and see what happens?"

He smiled. "Yeah, whatever you like," he whispered. He lifted his right hand from where it pressed to the door next to my head and ran his fingers over my cheek, a delicate caress. Then he cupped my jaw gently, most of his fingers behind my ear as one traced the sensitive lobe. Drawing his hand over my chin and cheek, he found my lips. His touch was so very light, teasing.

I closed my eyes, lips parting slightly at the warmth of his fingers upon me. I just wanted to feel this, let my senses drink in his careful ministrations.

"Your lips are amazing, so full and soft," he whispered, and he was so close I felt his hot breath upon my cheek. I let out a hot breath as well, thrilled by his words and warmth. "I can't wait to kiss them." He pressed two fingers to my lips as if in some mock kiss. "To trace my tongue over them." He outlined them with a finger once again. "To make you moan and let my tongue fill you when your mouth opens to me." One finger slid between my slightly parted lips, touching my teeth before drawing back and taking my bottom lip with it.

He was leaning close on my right side, his mouth close to my ear. "Do you want me to kiss you, Feather?"

"Yes," I breathed.

"I would like to hear you say it," he whispered, lips so close he was practically kissing my cheek.

"Kiss me, Tail. Claim my lips with yours and send those wonderful fingers... elsewhere."

He gave a breathy laugh before trailing kisses down my cheek to my lips. And when his mouth did press to mine, gentle and urging, his lips were supple and strong, brushing and playing, sucking and nibbling.

He took a half-step in, his body pressing lightly against mine. Taking his other hand off the door, it slid behind me, enfolding me in a strong embrace as the hand from my face traced down my side to my hip and remaining firm there.

When I'd asked for slow, I hadn't expected this level of attention and care. Already I was over the moon with Tail's performance. I pressed my body to his. One of my hands slid behind him and the other went to his head to press his lips harder upon mine as I warmed to his skillful touch.

He drew back and whispered, "Anything else you'd like my goddess?" His hot breath on my wetted lips sent a thrill through me. He was being oh-so-attentive. "Tell me your desires and I will fulfill them."

Oh, wow, definitely not a brash young man eager to get his cock wet.

Indeed, he seems so young, but I sense he is well versed in the ways of pleasure. I felt the thrill in Leoa's voice.

I certainly hope so.

So... what did I want? "I want you to undress us slowly, sensually, kissing me all over. I want you to get me so hot and worked up I'm begging for you. Can you do that?"

I could feel his arousal, the hard erection pressing against my belly. A part of me was already regretting asking him to take it slow. I was the needful one, aching for him, but still I restrained myself. I had a feeling Tail could really draw this out and make me feel amazing, and I wanted that... all of that.

"I can," he whispered.

I melted just a little at the heat of his voice, the soft tenor, the easy confidence.

Spirits, I hoped he could deliver as promised.

"But I wasn't done savoring your lips." His hand behind me rose up to the back of my head, combing close through my hair, as he pressed in again. This time I did moan as he kissed me, opening to him as he'd anticipated. His tongue was slow and savvy, tracing the insides of my lips before delving deeper to dance with mine. His hand on my hip slipped back and cupped the heaviness of my round bottom, digging his fingers in, just a little. My hips shifted of their own accord, rocking, feeling his hardness dig into my belly. I lifted my leg, sliding up his thigh and hitching it on his hip, my skirts riding up.

And when his lips finally left mine, he pressed them to my cheek. I closed my eyes as he moved over my face, gently and slowly, before returning to my lips. If he took as much time with the rest of me as he'd just taken with my face, I was sure I wouldn't be disappointed.

I don't think he's going to disappoint you, and I don't think you'll need to be doing much teaching for this one, Leoa whispered, and I could hear the passion she was feeling in the breathy cadence of her voice. I had to agree but couldn't respond. She let out a breathy laugh. *I'll shut up now and let you enjoy what is to come.*

I was sure she'd be enjoying it too.

His hand on my bottom pressed us closer as my hips continued to rock over that impressive erection of his. I heard the faint, breathy growl from him as he smiled, heat in his eyes. He moved the hand behind my head lower, slowly smoothing a path down my back to the other cheek of my buttocks, as he let out a breathy moan, feeling my curves. Then, his hands slid up, over my hips and waist, to the sides of my breasts. He stepped back, my leg falling off his hip and returning to stabilize me, weak as it was becoming. His gaze devoured me, as he gently pressed my breasts together. Then, he slid his hands over my bosom, a lingering caress, before moving down to the belt of my dress and undoing it. I wasn't even out of my dress yet and I felt so very desired, sexy, and alive.

"Yes," I breathed, needing to let him know he was making me feel so very wonderful.

His hands sought my breasts again, moving over them slowly, up to the top button on the front of the dress. He moved in again, strong lips on mine, kissing as he undid the top button. Then his fingers played around the collar of the dress and the small bit of newly exposed skin. Yup, he was taking his time, and I was loving every second of this precious attention. My skin tingled and responded, hot and flushed, as he traced his fingers upon me.

Another button... and he took a long moment to feather a light-fingered touch over my upper chest. The anticipation of him moving lower, uncovering more, his hands upon my skin was driving me crazy. I loved it.

Another button and a finger drew a 'V' dipping down into the top of my cleavage. I shivered. I opened my lips to his and put my hands behind his head to draw him closer, deeper as our tongues met and mingled again.

I lost count of the next few buttons until one of his hands was fully inside my dress, pressing hard against a soft breast. He ran the tips of his fingers over my nipple. One. By. One. And by the time his last finger had flicked that precious nub, it was high and hard.

I let out a groan of satisfied pleasure at his seeking touch and his lips left mine, pulling back with a hungry look on his face. "Your breasts are amazing," he whispered. "All of you is amazing. And I can't wait to feel more of you, but I'll keep taking my time, if you like."

A part of me wanted to tear off our clothes and jump into his arms, legs wrapped around him as I felt him plunge into me, but... I had asked for slow and that's what I would get. "I do like," I whispered. "Very much."

He grinned, moving back in to resume our kiss as his hands opened more buttons, slowly roaming over my breasts, then my stomach, then my belly and...

He stepped back again then, to push the dress off my arms. He moved behind me, kissing every inch of exposed skin as he slowly revealed more and more of my arms and back, until his lips were pressed to one palm, then the other.

I was half-naked, my dress settled on my round hips.

"You're pretty amazing yourself," I said, voice trembling just a little. "Most men would have had us fully undressed by now, even if they were 'taking it slowly.' You certainly know what you're doing."

He grinned at the compliment as he moved around in front of me again. "My brother and I were... sought after in our town. We're both... experienced lovers." He took a moment to simply drink me in, gaze wandering over my body. "I get the feeling the same is true of you?" he asked but didn't seem to really expect an answer. "I only hope I can live up to your high expectations."

And I did have high expectations. Davas had been a very attentive lover. He would— No! I shut that thought down and made sure I was still smiling at Tail. Hopefully he hadn't seen my momentary distraction.

Tail knelt and kissed my belly, hands firm on my bottom. He took his time, slowly roaming the expanse of my lower torso, before he ever-so-slowly pushed my dress down. Inch.

By. Inch. Until it was just barely clinging to the tops of my thighs.

I let out a gasping moan as he kissed just above my curls. I moved a hand down to the back of his head, feeling the low, tight curls of his black hair. He slowly kissed his way around a large thigh until I felt his lips brushing the top of my buttocks.

Oh, Spirits! Enough of this! I stepped away from him and pushed my dress off entirely, going to sit on my bed.

Tail knelt on the floor with a surprised look. "Are you begging for me, now?"

Pits yes!

"Not quite yet, but you're doing a really good job of getting me there. Now take your clothes off, slowly, and show me that body of yours." Some women didn't like to ask for what they wanted. They thought it too forward. I had no such qualms.

He rose and nodded. "As you wish, my goddess." He began to slowly unbutton his shirt.

"Do you call every woman a goddess?"

"No." He actually seemed to be trying to remember. "I don't think so. I've called some lovers *Princess* or *Lady*, but I'm fairly certain you're the first I've called a goddess."

He did indeed take his time undressing, making it a tease, using his hands to touch himself as he slowly removed his shirt, then his pants. Spirits, but he was well built. He wasn't big, but he had a wide chest and large rounded shoulders. His arms were well developed, and his abs were a perfect set of eight rolling hills, with a perfect V down into his black curls. He had a narrow waist and strong, rippling muscles on his legs. And then there was his erection, thick and proud and twitching with a heavy tip that got me wet just looking at it. Though, to be fair, Tail had done a good job of getting me wet before this.

Still, I wasn't begging yet. That surprised me a little. I was so hot and ready, but I also loved the anticipation of this slow and sensuous tease. And Tail, true to his word, continued with exactly that, since I hadn't told him to ravish me yet. He got to his knees, hands on my thighs, pushing them apart as he ducked low. Not many of the men I'd been with had explored my folds with their lips and tongue, and most of those who had, hadn't known what they were doing. I hoped Tail did.

I leaned back, tilting my hips up to give him access. He kissed my thighs first, moving in, slowly, until I felt the tip of his tongue brush my folds and I gasped. He licked slowly up one side and down the other and I felt myself open to him. Reaching down, I put my hands to his head as his tongue probed deeper still, and I moaned as a shiver of pleasure ran through me.

Oh yes, Tail knew very well what he was doing as he added in sure, strong lips, and tentative teeth, a bit of suction and lot of attention to the growing puddle that was my opening. And even as I wondered if he knew the female body well enough to seek the clitoris... his tongue flicked the hot bud. I gave a clipped cry at the spike of pleasure that brought. I was nearly there, nearly at the point of begging for that amazing erection of his.

He sucked upon my gloriously sensitive clit, tongue slowly flicking over it, and I shuddered, feeling the gripping heat of an orgasm building in my core. I groaned again, to urge him onward. Then his kisses moved over my belly once again and I almost whined at the lack of stimulation, but then his fingers took up the work at my opening, moving deftly over and inside me. And when, with two fingers, he reached up inside me to some place behind my clitoris, while using his thumb outside to stimulate that sensitive spot, I lost it. My body contracted with a small orgasm — a teasing release — and I was suddenly done with the slow and sensual play. I wanted him, all of him, inside me, hard and...

"Yes, now! I'm begging, please!"

My eyes had been clenched shut, but I opened them as I felt him shift. He leaned down, hands to either side of me, poised over me, that heavy cock slowly descending. He said a breathy, "My pleasure."

And I was sure it would be mine too.

CHAPTER 9

TAIL

By all the Spirits of the Mists! Feather was amazing!

I had been with many young women, but Feather was a true woman; all woman. And far more than that, unlike the others I'd been with, she knew exactly what she wanted and how she wanted it and let me know how I was doing as I did it. It was amazing to have that feedback, to know when and how she wanted me. Most women were too shy, but Feather was nothing of the sort.

I'd never wanted a woman more in my life. This drawn-out session of fun foreplay had my cock aching to the point of strain and pain. And when she finally said those magic words: *Yes, now! I'm begging, please!* I was so very ready to fulfill her desire.

I am surprised you lasted this long, Isoa, my Lumani, said. They were a ball of white and gold illuminating the room behind me. Their voice was filled with the heated intensity of desire I was feeling. Even though we weren't Bonded yet, they felt what I felt. I ignored them for now. My mind was elsewhere.

I was leaning over, taking her all in before the ragged

passion I knew was to come. I lowered my hips and let my cock slide around her folds. She moaned, her hips rising, dipping me in just a little more. I was so ragingly hard and she so ready and wet that I slid into her easily, her folds seemed to pull me in. There was a bit of tension as my tip slipped into her, then she was all wet warmth, welcoming me inside her.

"Oh, Spirits!" she cried out. "More!" But even though I knew we were both ready for the 'more' she'd requested, I didn't want to ruin my moment with this amazing woman. I wanted to worship at the sacred altar of this goddess for as long as I could. So, I began slow, shallow thrusts. I hiked one leg up onto her bed for added support, so I could regain the use of my hands, massaging her full, womanly thighs.

Your patience is commendable in one so young. I'm not certain I could have waited so long. Isoa seemed surprised again.

I'm eighteen, not so young, and I've had a lot of experience with women to prepare for this glorious moment. And it was a good thing too; for some reason I didn't want to disappoint this amazing woman before me.

I caught her gaze, dark eyes hooded; desperate. "I said you could take me," she breathed. "You don't have to take it slow anymore." Her voice was strained, tremulous.

"I don't have to," I said with a grin. "But I want to. I want to savor every glorious moment with you. I've never been with anyone like you, and just in case this is the only chance I get, I want to make the most of it."

She laid her head back and gave a gasping laugh. "Given how amazing and patient and — Spirits, yes — you've been. Something tells me a second chance is in your future."

That was the best news I'd ever heard.

Do you love her? Isoa was a new Lumani; they'd only had

one host before me and were still limited in their knowledge of the world. It could be annoying at times.

I am loving her, there's a difference. Though, I did love her. I loved everything about her. I knew it was infatuation still, but something told me this feeling could easily grow into something deeper and more lasting. But that was for later. Now was for giving her the heights of ecstasy.

I leaned forward and swept my hands up to her breasts, those magnificent mounds, feeling their soft warmth and the immediate responsiveness of her large areolae and tall nipples. As I leaned forward, I slid myself fully into her, feeling the heat of her surround me until my body was pressed hard to hers.

She breathed a whimpering, "Yes!" drawing out the word.

I began full strokes of my cock, harder, surer. I knew we were both getting so very close to our peaks and wanted nothing more than to give her that epitome of bliss.

I tuned out any further comments or questions from Isoa and focused on Feather, on our joining of pleasure.

"Harder," she breathed.

I kept one hand on a gloriously full breast, the other going to the bed for more leverage, fisting the sheets as I gave three hard thrusts, slapping myself into her. And that had been exactly what she'd wanted. I felt her body tense as she cried out wordlessly. She raised her legs to wrap around me, tightly, drawing me closer. Her entrance contracted, squeezing me. She bucked so hard she knocked my leg off the bed. I lost all leverage from my legs, but she didn't mind. I kept myself deep inside her, hardly moving as she came around me. Instead, I dug my fingers into her breast, gripping hard. She arched her back with another cry of pleasure, her hips rocking as she took more of her bliss from me.

My cock was still aching and full. Even with her pussy milking me, I hadn't come. I'd thought that would be it for me, but instead the exquisite ache of my near-orgasm pressed upon me. Apparently, I wanted more.

When her body finally relaxed a little and she'd released her legs from around me, she heaved a heavy breath. "That was amazing!"

"I'm not done," I whispered and she looked up at me, eyes wide.

"No?"

"No."

She gave me a sloppy, silly grin. "Well, I am more than pleased with your work so far. You've given me everything I wanted. So, I think it's your turn. What do you want?"

I knew exactly what I wanted.

I leaned over until the smooth skin of her cheek pressed against mine as I whispered into her ear. "I want you. I want all of you, Feather. You're the most amazing woman I've ever known. I want to make you come over and over again." I drew my cock out of her, feeling the cool air around it as she gasped and mewled in protest. "Roll over," I commanded.

I stood and let her move, rolling over. She pulled her legs up under her on the bed and pushed out her butt, waving it slightly. "Is this what you want?" she teased. I could see the tight pucker of her rear entrance and the wet folds of her amazing opening. I pushed myself back into her pussy, grabbing her hips to drive myself in deep.

"Oh, Precious Spirits of the Mists!" she breathed. "Oh, yes!" Her body shook and shivered; I knew she was oh-so-sensitive now.

I leaned forward, running my hands down the dark-honey-brown skin of her back, then slipped them around front. "I want you up," I said. She rose, with my help, until she was kneeling on the bed, butt pushed back into me, back arched, hands out on the wall on the other side of the bed.

"Like this?" she asked and I had to admit, this was perfect; she was perfect.

"Oh, Spirits, yes," I breathed, so near to my release. I nearly came then, but I held, pained and swollen with near-to-bursting fullness inside her.

I ran my hands up over her breasts, feeling their weight and fullness for a moment, savoring them. Feather's were the largest tits I'd ever seen. And as much as I didn't care about a woman's size. I had to admit, these heavenly orbs were stunning. I massaged them for a moment as Feather moaned, whined, and groaned. Then... I began driving myself into her, hard and relentless with need. I lost myself. She was crying out, wordless with bliss as my own ecstasy rose, then crashed down over me like a massive tidal wave. Quickly moving my hands back to her hips, I slammed myself deep as I exploded within her and we both cried out as I finally, blessedly, found my release. Her opening clenched tight around me. I could feel the pounding of her heart through that connection, pulling me, drawing me in and prolonging my orgasm. I had never felt such a powerful and full release as this. I felt like I couldn't stop, and the way she shivered and moaned, I didn't think she wanted me to, either.

Eventually she pushed herself off the wall and leaned back against me as I held her. With one arm around her stomach to keep her close, I let the other hand stroke her side: from glorious thighs, over round hips and the curve of her waist up to magnificent breasts.

She leaned her head back on my shoulder and though the angle was a bit awkward we shared some playful kisses and heated looks. When she could speak, she whispered, "I've had some amazing sex in my life and I have to say this was up there as one of the best things I've ever felt."

"That is until next time," I breathed with a mock-arrogant laugh.

"Oh, Spirits!" She quivered and laughed.

We stayed like that, pressed together for some time. We continued to kiss and nibble each other's lips. It seemed to take forever for me to come down from this high, but eventually both of our bodies grew weary.

Once I'd removed myself, we lay together for a while on her bed, simply exploring each other with soft-brushing fingers.

Will you marry her? Isoa asked, still so unknowing in the ways of humans.

Probably not. Though, in this moment, I couldn't think of being anywhere but with her. But she and Dawn had made it clear, this was fun, play, nothing more.

But you have 'loved' her.

Physical love, yes,

Ah, and there is a difference between physical and emotional love? I understand.

I hoped so. Yet… I knew I could so very easily lose myself in this woman.

"Is your brother as good as you?" she asked. She looked away, perhaps thinking that wasn't what she should be asking a man.

"He's my twin; he's as good as me. Depending on the day, he's better."

She looked back at me, an odd smile on her face. "Would you care if I screamed louder for him?"

I shook my head. "You're an amazing woman and deserve only amazing men pleasuring you, serving your every whim. If he gives you greater joy than I did, I'll be glad." He chuckled. "And it just means I'll have to make you scream all the louder the next time."

She quivered again with a glazed-over look in her eyes and that sloppy grin. "I already can't wait."

There came a quiet knock on the door.

"And there he is," I said, then leaned in for a soft kiss on those full dark lips and one last stroke of my hand along her side before rising and dressing quickly.

I didn't know what Dawn would be like but she'd be nothing like Feather, of that I was sure. It wouldn't be better or worse, just... different. And I was very much looking forward to that, as well as my next time with Feather.

Blessed Spirits, I didn't know why they'd chosen me. These two amazing women could have had any man here, but they'd picked me and I would forever be thankful to the Spirits for that.

CHAPTER 10

DAWN

THEY WERE TWINS, THERE WAS NO DOUBT ABOUT IT. WHEN they had climbed in through my window, both in their Silverveil uniforms, I'd not been able to tell them apart. The only difference was the color of their Lumani: Tail's was a large ball of white and gold. He'd left, sneaking out to Feather's room, leaving me with Agate. This twin's Lumani was a ball of deep, dark purples and blues.

"I don't believe we've met," I said.

The beautiful man smiled, full lips spreading upon that exquisite dark-skinned face. "No. I'm Agate." He held out a hand and I took it. He lifted my fingers to his lips for a brief kiss, all the while his dark eyes took me in hungrily. "And might I say, my brother's description of you didn't do you justice, you are exquisite."

Was I? I knew my raven hair and pale skin were a stark contrast and set off my features. My sunrise-gold eyes were also unusual for any non-Fey. I'd have described myself as striking, not exquisite.

I must have blushed as his eyes widened. "Oh, and that blush on those fair cheeks of yours is enough to bring a man to his knees." He then fell to his knees. With my hand still held in his he clasped his other hand over it. "I cannot believe my incredible fortune to be here with you."

He certainly had a lot of flowery words. Usually that wouldn't affect me, but there was something so heartfelt in how he spoke. It was getting my blood pumping just a little quicker. So, I stepped in, pulling my hand from his to put my hands on his shoulders. It was pretty much impossible for a man to be shorter than I was and I liked this position for him, since it meant he came to roughly my shoulders.

It also meant he was staring right at my tits.

But there I hesitated.

Agate was handsome. He had the build of a man, not a boy, with brown skin and dark eyes. I did want to fool around tonight, but the real truth was... I hardly knew what that meant. I'd had all of one sexual encounter in my life and didn't really know what it was like to be wooed. I wasn't even sure if I wanted wooing or just a release, feeling all of this sexy man in and on me? How did I say that while not letting him know how inexperienced or naïve I actually was?

You like to be in control, Amya noted, floating off in a corner of the room.

And?

Perhaps try... letting down your walls, being vulnerable. Just tell him the truth.

I...

It would be a pretty radical thing for such a controlling woman to do, wouldn't it?

Amya had me there.

I sighed. "You have a lot of pretty words," I said, our gazes locked. "I'll be honest with you. I don't know what I want tonight. I know I don't want any lasting relationship, only some fun. But... I don't know whether I want you to just hold me and kiss me or stick your cock in my pussy and make me come until I pass out." He smiled at that, raising a brow, but let me go on. This was the hard part. "I... am not particularly experienced. I've... ah... visited a brothel and I —" I laughed realizing what I was saying as I said it. "— know the *ins and outs*, but I've never really had a tryst like this before and want to experience... everything. But I don't even know what *everything* means."

He raised a finger to my lips, silencing me softly. Then that same finger traced down, over my chin and neck and his hand settled between my breasts, not fondling but firm. He pressed there for a moment. "Listen to your heart, Dawn," he whispered, and between the soft words and where his hand was, my heart was certainly trying to say something, pounding like I'd run a mile. "I've had a few encounters with women, some more experienced than others. Let me tell you what I want."

I nodded, curious.

His hand on my chest became just a finger, tracing a line back up, making my skin alight with pleasant tingling where it passed. It returned to my face, then brushed my lips again. "I want to kiss these small, cherry-blossom lips of yours. I want to savor their sweetness before moving my kisses to that faint blush upon your cheeks, or the taut upturn of your ears. I want to nibble your neck as my hands caress every other part of you. And I'd be happy if we did no more than that." But then a new heat kindled behind his dark eyes. "But... I'd be happier still if you wanted more."

That all sounded quite interesting.

I took control again. "Enough with the pretty words, kiss me," I said and leaned down to press my lips to his. They were full and parted at my touch, inviting me in deeper.

True to his word, he sucked and played, savoring our kiss. His tongue traced my mouth before lancing inside me, beckoning my tongue to rouse and revel. Strong arms enfolded me, pulling me close as playful turned to heated. I slid my hands up from his shoulder to his head, pressing him closer for a long moment before... I became very curious what his kisses would feel like elsewhere.

He was already at just the right height and my tits were aching for some attention, so I pulled him off me and let my head loll back, eyes closed as I moaned softly. I wanted to *feel* all of this. I pressed his face into my cleavage, arms wrapping around his head. His full lips pressed to the sheer fabric of my shirt, covering my breasts with kisses, even sensing my hardening nipples and playfully arousing them to stiffened peaks.

My breath shuddered when he pulled back. He whispered, "Despite what you said, you certainly seem to know what you want."

And I did now. "I want you to make me feel... even more amazing than this, if that's possible."

"Oh... it is." He leaned in to kiss the exposed skin high on my chest, where my shirt was open. His breath was hot on my skin as he elaborated. "I'll thrill you slowly until you're begging for me to claim you."

"I don't beg."

He laughed. "Demanding for me to claim you, then."

Sounded good to me. "Shut up and do it."

His lips sought my neck while his hands moved from their embrace to caress as well. From where he was, on his knees, he could reach almost to the floor. His hands stroked the full length of my legs, over my tight pants. And when they found the taut hills of my ass, they lifted and grasped. This coincided with our lips coming together again and I moaned into his mouth, which seemed only to thrill him all the more.

Then those skilled hands slid around, caressing over my shirt, up my belly to cup my breasts, tender and careful, massaging my small sensitive mounds until I was boiling over with desire. My body was pulsing with heat, radiating out from my core in waves.

Enough of this. I reached down and began to unbutton his shirt, hoping he got the hint. He did and his masterful fingers easily flicked over my buttons to open my shirt down to my navel. Large, strong hands with thick, kneading fingers slid over my burning skin to encompass my small breasts. This time he wasn't soft and massaging. He gripped hard, pushing my swells up as my rigid nipples dug into his palms. I hadn't known I'd wanted it that rough until he'd done it and I gasp-moaned with a full-body shutter which pulled his lips off mine.

"Yes," I breathed, our gazes locked. "More, like that."

He grinned and obliged. His lips joined his hands. He gripped the circumference of my breast and brought his lips to my nipple, sucking, plucking, even raking his teeth over the tight flesh and it was... amazing. I hadn't thought a woman could come just from nipple stimulation, but I felt a wave of needful, clenching bliss in my gut. My pussy ached, yearning to be touched. I didn't know what I wanted more in that moment: for Agate to keep working on my tits or go... lower. I just let myself enjoy all of the thrilling sensations as I stroked his chest under his shirt, exploring that wide expanse of heavy muscle.

While his lips roamed over my aching breasts, he completely removed my shirt. I did the same with him, pulling his off. His hands slid down to settle on the top of my pants as he drew back and caught my gaze again. "What does my mistress command next?"

Why did he have to ruin it by asking? But then, in a flash, I knew what I wanted. I drew back and sat on the bed. "Get up and take off your pants," I said.

He rose with that same cocky grin. Then he... slowly... unbuttoned his pants and teased them down. My heart lurched, eyes going wide when his cock leaped out to freedom. I swallowed hard. It was... significant indeed, thick and full, with a heavy, swollen head. I reached out and grabbed it. *This* was what I'd wanted. I Pulled him closer and he stumbled forward as I stroked that magnificent cock. The man I'd been with in Weijin had not been as big as Agate — in every aspect — but still very skilled. I wasn't sure what Agate could do with this much larger cock, but I was suddenly *very* curious. But first I just wanted to see it, watch it, feel it. I felt the strong twitch and throb of the shaft as I stroked it, noticed the small pool of glistening wetness at his opening. I stroked down and off, cupping his heavy sack, feeling its weight, grasping it and playing before returning to his twitching-ever-harder shaft.

If you'd wanted to know more about the male phallus, I could have filled you in, Amya said, a bit clinically.

Not in the way I want to be filled in.

Ah... no, I suppose not.

And please don't interrupt us again.

Understood.

"Are you going to play with it all night?" Agate asked, voice strained.

"And what if I did?" I looked up and made sure our gazes were locked as I leaned forward and tasted his cock with my tongue, tracing it around his heavy tip.

Agate was struggling, I could see that, a bonfire behind

his eyes, swallowing hard, jaw tense. "Don't *you* want... anything more?" he gasped. I wrapped my lips around his tip, letting my saliva warm him as my tongue slowly flicked over him. He gasped again, then suddenly... he grinned. "How would you feel about... something... different?" he asked, suddenly back in control of himself again.

I was curious. *Different?*

This should be interesting, Amya said, curious. It was the goal of all Lumani to seek new and different things, all aspects of the human experience. *Sorry, I'll shut up now.*

Drawing back from his cock, my saliva stringing along between us, I smiled. "I like different. I'm all for new and exciting." I shivered as I said it. With my limited experience I got the feeling when Agate said different, he meant... *different.*

"Oh, I was hoping you'd say that. The girls from my town were nice, but they weren't that adventurous. I've been wanting to try some things... if you're willing," he added that end bit quickly.

"I'm willing," I said, thrilled at the unknown possibilities of what he was suggesting. Apparently, I'd moved past my questions about what I wanted. I just wanted him. My pussy clenched and throbbed for more. I knew I'd not be satisfied with just playing any longer.

I let go of his cock and leaned back on my bed, thrusting out my chest just a little. "What did you have in mind?"

He stood back to give me a bit of room. "First..." His eyes roamed over me, devouring. "Take off *your* pants." He licked his lips, expectant, as I rose.

I made a show of it, like he had. I undid the ties and slowly inched them down. He unabashedly stroked his cock as he watched me and I loved what I seemed to do for him. When I stepped out of my pants, we stood before each other naked. His dark skin gleamed in the lamp-light, and the glow of our Lumani. I felt my legs go just a little weak, like I had that afternoon gazing at his brother. But this time I had the added pleasure of seeing all of his rolling muscles and the fullness of his twitching cock.

As that exploratory silence stretched out between us, my heart thundered with curious expectation at what was to come.

CHAPTER 11

DAWN

AGATE SWOOPED IN, EASILY PICKING ME UP, HANDS ON MY sides and kissed me quickly. "You don't know how much I've been waiting for this. You're amazing! And you're so... I just... there's something about you, it radiates from you, pulling me in and... Maybe it's those eyes, like the morning sun," he breathed.

More flowery words, when what I really wanted was to find out what he meant by *different*. Yet, I didn't mind the words so much this time. He was growing on me.

He put me down and went to the bed, lying on his side, bottom leg slightly out, top leg slightly back. "Now you do the same, lay like this, but... the other way," he said. I climbed onto the bed and began to lean down when he chuckled. "No, the other way."

It took me a moment to understand, but I nodded. We weren't going to be head-to-head, I'd be upside-down to him. I lay down, my head on his outstretched thigh... that pulsing cock suddenly very close.

"Yeah, just rest your head on my thigh," he said. At the same time, he pulled my bottom thigh under his head. That put him... oh! So, we'd be doing this together, each pleasuring the other with our mouths to start. I felt his tongue trace my folds and gave a shuddering gasp.

I could get to like this.

I grasped his thick cock in my hand and stroked it again. It was slightly awkward at this angle, but I brought it to my lips and flicked my tongue over his tip. It was his turn to gasp. He was being so very intent and insistent between my legs. His arm curled around my upper leg, holding it aloft as his face pressed deeper, putting glorious pressure on me. I wanted to return the favor. Once again, I took the tip of his cock fully into my mouth, swirling my tongue around it, clamping my lips closed to suck gently upon him. I felt him swell and pulse in response, hearing his groans as he continued to work his magic lips on my—

I had to pull him out of my mouth as I gasped. He'd found my clit, lapping with his tongue, sending my body into twitching convulsions with each stroke.

And suddenly that aching need in my gut was stoked to a raging inferno. I moaned a long and needful sound as he drove me higher into bliss.

He gave a long, drawn-out grunt, sounding pained. I wondered what I was doing to get that reaction. I didn't even have him in my mouth, I was just holding... oh... I'd clamped my hand around his cock. With my Fey strength, it must have been intense for him. I released him a little, and he relaxed. I began stroking him again, slowly getting the feel for this odd position, especially liking what he was doing for me. I was quickly becoming a quivering, wet mess down there and wanted to make sure he felt the same. With tongue and teeth, I teased his tip, loving how his cock pulsed in my grasp and hearing Agate's corresponding grunts and moans.

Then, one of his hands slipped up to rub my clit as his tongue slid inside me.

That was it for me. I came... hard, body tensing, muscles clenching as I cried out around his cock. I wanted him to come too, stroking him viciously as I sucked hard on his tip, but he didn't release.

And after a moment, I didn't care. I rolled back — only half paying attention to stroking him — as my orgasm took over. It shook me, tense and trembling through me before relaxing every muscle in my body, filling me with a warm and pleasant tingling.

I heard Agate say: "I'm glad you liked that."

It was hard for me to form words. My throat was dry, my breath coming in heavy gasps. "You... need...?"

He laughed. "Oh no, not yet. I have a few more positions in mind before that."

Spirits!

"What's... next?" I asked. I wanted more.

"There's another position I've always wanted to try. I honestly don't know what it will be like, but if you're up for something different...?" His breath was also catching as I continued to casually stroke his length.

"Just... tell me... where you... want me." I was slowly regaining my voice.

"Oh, Spirits, you're amazing!" He drew away and lay back on the bed, bringing his legs together. "Straddle me but facing my feet."

That was an interesting start. I moved over him. For a moment I just sat on his stomach, facing his feet, with his cock once again in my hands stroking him. Then I levered myself up and played his cock around in my messy, dripping folds. I was more than ready for him, and desperately curious how he'd feel inside me. He was so thick! I slowly eased myself down on him, shuddering with mini-orgasms as he filled me, making me feel tight when I really wasn't. And when I finally settled fully onto him, there was an exquisite pressure so very deep within me, which prompted a hard, body-clenching orgasm. I mewled and moaned as the intense and powerful bliss shot out from my core to all parts of my body. Agate's hands came to my waist, holding me in place as I trembled through the release.

"You done already?" he asked, joking.

Blessed Spirits, I could be. "Just... getting started," I gasped, slowly rocking myself on that magnificent length of his. "Is this it?" I asked. If it was, it had already worked for me.

"Not yet."

Oh Spirits, there's more?

I felt him rise up behind me, curving his abs around me to what must have been an awkward sitting position. He slid his arms up, caressing my stomach, then up to my breasts, cupping the soft swells as he kissed my back. "Now, ease yourself forward," he said. "Slowly, down till you're almost on your stomach, leaning on your arms on the bed." He opened his legs and I leaned forward, hands on his legs first, moving down, until I could touch the bed.

"Oh, wow!" I gasped, his cock was pressing back within me the further I leaned forward and that was doing some wonderful things. I leaned down on my arms, stomach hovering over the bed. Looking back, he was half-sitting, propped up on his arms. "Like this?" I asked, then gave my ass a little shake.

"Yeah..., ooh, yes!" he said. "You've got all the control here." He sat up a bit so he could put his hands on the sides of my hips. "You can lift a little or rock back and forth, what-ever works for you." He used his hands to move me a little as he spoke. "You'll keep me on the edge of tension, while doing whatever you need to get yourself off." His hands slid around to grasp my buttocks. "And I have some fun things to work with as well." I felt a sudden pressure on my other entrance as he played and pressed a finger into me. This surprise stimulation blasted through me, far more pleasurable than I'd expected and I bucked with another sudden orgasm. I gasped wordless noises as the bliss took me, rolling through me, seizing and releasing muscles all the way up till even my hair was tingling.

"You like that?" he asked, playfully.

I couldn't even fully respond. It took me a long moment to gasp, "Yes!"

The man who I'd been with at the pleasure-house in Weijin had brought me to such heights of pleasure but hadn't done any of the curious and new things Agate was trying. It opened up a whole world of pleasure for me, and suddenly I wanted to repay this intensity of ecstasy I was feeling. So, I did as he'd mentioned, getting my knees under me I bobbed up and down on his erection as fast as this odd position would allow. I heard his low, moaning hum of pleasure. I added to this a soft rocking motion, making sure not to strain him too much, vigorously working over him. And I could feel the intensity of his need as his cock throbbed and swelled.

"Yes," he breathed. "Yes! You're... oh!"

He had two fingers inside my other entrance now, thrusting and moving in time with me. I was quickly building to another orgasm and lost myself to my thrusting upon him for a long moment, seeking only my own need, feeling it build and build until...

I clamped down on his cock and fingers as I rose up on stiff arms, finding just the right position for the next immense peak to thrum through me. I didn't even know what noise I was making, I wasn't really paying attention, just focusing on this trembling bliss surging through me, ringing me like a bell, over and over and over. It was so powerful I actually bucked completely off his cock, immediately feeling the loss.

I rolled over onto my back, tears in my eyes at the extremity of joy I'd just felt.

"I see that worked for you," he said with a laugh.

"I... yes..." I couldn't speak more than one word at a time between gasping breaths.

He leaned over me, lying beside me to kiss a breast, sucking on my nipple, which brought another spike of joy.

"Did you...?" I asked, and he caught my meaning.

"Not yet."

"Spirits, just... take what you need, I'm..." I lost my mind to bliss, arching my back as he sucked on that nipple again. Yup, I could come just from nipple stimulation alone.

He lifted away. "What if I just want to keep you trapped here in this moment?"

Spirits, that would be the most amazing thing I'd ever experienced, but I knew it wouldn't last forever. I grabbed his face in both hands and brought it up to me, mashing his lips to mine in a violent, needful kiss. Then I met his eyes as I drew back, knowing I was a mess of intensity at the moment. "Take me. Take what you need. I want you to feel like I do!" Then I grinned. "Besides, you still have another woman to please tonight!"

He matched my grin. "She won't be anything like you."

No, she wouldn't. She'd be—

I lost that thought as he reached down to stroke my quivering folds. Then he shifted, moving over me, opening my legs wide to get between them. He leaned down to kiss my lips, then neck, each breast, then lower as he slowly drew himself back to a sitting position. His strong hands grabbed my thighs pulling me to him, lifting me a little then... I felt the oh-so-wonderful fullness of his erection press upon me. I was wet and gaping as he pushed his tip inside me. That brought another spike of joy, and I lost myself in that moment as he continued to adjust things. He brought my legs together, both ankles on one of his shoulders. He pressed my thighs to each other and suddenly he felt massive inside me. I'd thought myself open and welcoming, but now I felt more compressed, tighter, and it was wonderful. He pulled me close, ensuring he was fully inside me. Then he gripped my hips, fingers digging in.

Our gazes met and he grinned. "You asked for this," he said with a wink then began a hard and needful thrusting. If I had thought my thrusting upon him had been good, his passionate and possessive pounding was so much more amazing! My world exploded. I felt my back lift from the bed, then my shoulders, pressing my head back into the mattress, arms to the sides grasping sheets as I writhed with bliss. My mouth gaped in a silent scream of ecstasy.

He leaned forward, his hands sliding up to my breasts, clasping them as his grunting escalated and I knew he was close. He swelled inside me, then with a hard final thrust I felt his explosive release as he cried out. I was so far gone into bliss, I floated in a place of quivering joy as he twitched and pulsed in the throes of his orgasm.

Then, he was shifting my legs down as he leaned forward, putting his weight upon me as the last of his release brought aftershocks of bliss to us both.

It was a long time before either of us could speak.

"That was... amazing!" I said, still a little winded, mouth dry.

It certainly was. I like this one, can we keep him? Amya asked, voice quivering with pleasure.

No, this was just play, besides we haven't been with his brother yet.

Oh! Right, I'll reserve judgement for now. I could tell Amya was joking, but still, it was curious how quickly he'd wanted to claim Agate.

"And... different as promised," I added.

He laughed, his cock shuddering inside me, and that caused a whole new set of wonderful sensations, which spiked my pleasure once again.

I couldn't imagine how his brother was going to top this.

But I was suddenly very eager to find out.

CHAPTER 12

AGATE

My body hummed with life and energy as I kissed Dawn goodbye and quickly dressed to sneak out of her room. I'd never felt this alive before!

I was trembling. Dawn had been amazing, so powerful of spirit, so adventurous and willing to experiment sexually with me. That alone had made tonight glorious! None of the young women from back in Halena Village had been that bold in bed. They'd given me, and my brother, a solid education on the basics of sex and the female form. For my brother Erran — no, his name was Tail now — that had been enough. But for me, I'd wanted to know so much more. I'd expanded my... education through the acquisition of some hard-to-find books. Luckily, being the son of Nobles, I'd had the resources and connections to get them. There was so much more I wanted to try, and Dawn, at least, seemed willing to try it with me.

And I still had another engagement tonight, and my anticipation to be with Feather, also contributed to my slightly shaky state. I only had my brother's description of the woman, but still, she sounded fascinating.

I was curious, when I Chose you, about your many thoughts on such sensual things, Eluei said softly, feminine voice silken and smooth. *I thought them initially only the lustiness of a young male, but I see now... you are so much more. Your desire for experimentation is enticing. I love it. I do certainly hope you get to experiment some more.*

As do I. I had only just learned how to speak to her in my head. *With luck we'll both get an interesting education on the intricacies of every possible sexual encounter.*

I do certainly hope so. I have never shied away from sex. I was always a little lusty. I think we will be a good pair, you and me.

That was my hope as well.

I paused before knocking on Feather's door. From Erran's — no Tail's — description of Feather, she was fuller of figure, but that didn't mean adventurous. I'd have to see what she was into. She might also be a bit fatigued from her time with my brother, he liked to linger with ladies, stretching the limits of their endurance. So, I might need to be a bit gentler and patient with her.

And your capacity to delay your desire is... stunning. Eluai's silken tones slid through my mind. *A few of my previous hosts were men, but mostly I've Bonded with women. And as a woman, most of the men I've been with have been in far too much of a hurry to gratify themselves. You are a gem, Agate, a true marvel.*

I'll show Feather just how much of a marvel I can be.

Then by all means, please continue. I'm burning with desire to feel every aching moment.

I smiled and knocked softly on the door of room twelve. There were some soft sounds from within before Tail — I got his name right this time! — answered the door. We smiled, seeing each other. It was an unconscious thing, a strange phenomenon with twins, seeing your duplicate before you — at least for us — always made us smile.

Tail closed the door softly behind him.

"She is amazing!" he breathed, and I could see the truth of it in his dark eyes and his broad, awed, grin. "So full of life and passion. And she knows what she wants. I've never met a woman so experienced and certain. I hope I didn't tire her out too much for you."

"I have ways of rousing women," I said. "And as for Dawn, she may not have the depth of experience, but she is... intoxicating. She exudes a presence which pulls you in. Oh, but she is small though, so she may be a bit sore."

"Rough, were you?" Tail cocked a brow.

"Eventually."

Tail chuckled. "Yeah, so were we." He patted my shoulder. "I told her you were better than I was, go prove me right."

"I will," I said a bit surprised by this. Tail and I had participated in a friendly rivalry in all things since we'd been boys. For him to so freely admit that I was better, was slightly out of character. But then I realized: by telling her I was better, now I had to be, and if I wasn't, I'd let her down. *Well played brother.*

I slipped into the room, carefully and quietly closing the door... and there she was. Feather lounged on her bed, some stray sheets over her, but not covering anything important. Almost instantly my cock was rock hard.

Oh Blessed Spirits! I would kill for her figure! Eluei's voice was hushed and awed. *You are a lucky man.* She floated off to a corner of the room.

I am.

"My brother's description didn't do you justice," I

breathed as I drew closer, coming to kneel at the side of the bed.

She smiled a catlike grin as I let my eyes roam that magnificent body, from waves of auburn hair to intense dark pools of her eyes, and full lips. I marveled at her full, generous breasts — with large dark areolae and aroused nipples — slender, curving waist and round hips. Her legs were full and womanly.

"Your brother called me a goddess, what do you think?" she said, voice low, purring. It was clear she was in the sensual daze after mind-blowing sex.

"He was right." I gestured to myself. "And I am already kneeling at your altar." I looked into those deep, dark eyes. "He also said you know what you like and aren't afraid to tell a man. What do you wish of me?" I quickly added. "I am familiar with a few unique positions, if you'd like something... new?"

She raised a dark brow and smiled, rounding those tawny cheeks. "Oh?" She relaxed back from her reclining position and stretched, squirming a little, and I couldn't help but be mesmerized by the innate sensuality in every movement. It stirred something deep within me. I *needed* to pleasure her, please her. She *was* a goddess, compelling my devotion.

"Your brother did a good job of pleasing me. I'm feeling all dopey and relaxed. What sort of ... encounter would you recommend where you do all the work to please your goddess?"

"Well, there are—"

"I don't care what the choices are, you pick one, and describe it to me, in aching detail." She drew out those last few words. She wanted me to stimulate her mind first, did she?

I could do that.

I also loved her surety and confidence.

Oh yes, I like her. You need to give her your all, Agate, for her, for me, for all women. Eluei must have been feeling my arousal already; she sounded like she was well gone to passion.

I will.

"Might I share your altar, goddess?" I asked.

"Of course," she said patting the small bed.

I climbed up onto the bed, lying on my side, precariously close to the edge, to give her all the room. I wracked my brain for a position I wanted to try, which would indeed be 'all me' as she desired.

Oh yes... I had one.

"Might I caress the goddess while I tell her of her impending pleasure?"

"You may," she said with a light giggle. I could tell she liked playing up her goddess nature. I reached a hand down to her face, brushing some sweat-dampened hair off and behind her ear before leaning down to kiss her forehead... then her lips. She was instantly responsive, mouth opening, one hand coming to my head to draw me down to her in a long and sensuous kiss. My hand traced her neck, then down over one shoulder, finding her other hand and interlocking our fingers for a moment of connection. Then I drew my hand over her belly, starting to trace patterns. She let out a few soft moans to encourage me and was already squirming with desire by the time my lips lifted away.

"Has my goddess..." I slid my hand down between her legs, past her slick folds to the puckered bud of her rear opening. "...ever had a man here?"

Oh! Interesting, Eluei purred. *Yes. As a man, I was with other men at times and I can vouch for the... satisfaction of having a cock back there.*

Good to know.

She shuddered, I didn't know if it was from my touch brushing past her loins or my suggestion. "No," she whispered. "And if you're anything like your brother, I don't know if you'd fit." I sensed her trepidation, her hesitation, the curiosity and doubt in her voice.

I brought my hand up to a pocket in my pants and drew out a small vial of oil. "I have something that will help with that. Yes, I am as large as my brother, but I believe this will work." Then, I went into the 'aching detail' she'd requested. "First, I will oil myself, stroking the liquid onto my rigid erection. Then, I will massage you with oil, slowly working my fingers into you, oiling you inside and out. This will bring some initial pleasure but will only be the beginning. When I enter you, I'll take my time, making sure the oil is doing its job... as I fill you... inch... by... inch, slick and slow, until I've filled you in a way unlike anything you've ever felt before. I will thrust, gently and slowly, as you rest. My hands will caress you, with easy access to your wonderous breasts and the sensitive miracle at your loins. I will pleasure you until you are delirious with bliss and only when you command will I find my release. I believe you will find this very stimulating indeed."

I find just your words stimulating enough! Oh... I can't wait!

Feather still looked a little trepidatious. "If I don't find it stimulating, I'll tell you," she said.

"Please do. I would never wish to make my goddess uncomfortable."

"Then... proceed."

I rose from the bed to quickly strip off my things and loved how those dark eyes of hers devoured me. As she watched, I dabbed out some of the oil in my vial and used my fingers to spread it over my cock, until I was glistening in the candlelight. I stroked myself slowly, letting her watch. Her mouth hung open just a little and whether consciously or not, she reached down and began stroking herself as well.

I felt Eluei's hum of pleasure as I caressed myself. But she said nothing, knowing when to keep quiet. She'd simply enjoy everything we were both about to feel.

"Roll to your side, my goddess," I said as I mounted the bed again. She rolled away from me and I slid in behind her, close and low. I lifted her upper leg, positioning it so it was forward a little bent at the knee. Then I began my ministrations, pouring out dabs of oil to begin massaging around her entrance, my slick fingers dancing around that sensitive spot and slowly probing inside.

I felt her tremble and sigh out a shuddering breath.

I kissed her back. "Pleasure, pain, or uncertainty, my goddess?"

"So far, only pleasure."

"Good."

I added more and more of my small vial of oil, dipping deeper into her, first one finger, then two, then three. And with each addition she'd shiver a bit more and whisper, "pleasure," to let me know how I was doing. Once she was starting to open, like a blossoming flower, I positioned my cock, pressing against the quivering opening.

"Ready?" I asked.

"Yes," she said, voice trembling.

I carefully pressed into her. I was thick, yes, but I knew she could take me. She gasped, louder and louder before letting out a long, "Ohhh!" once my tip was fully inside her.

"Pleasure," she whimpered. "You were right! Pleasure, Pleasure!"

"There's more of me," I said mischievously.

"Oh, Spirits! Really? You feel so huge and deep already!"

I slid a hand — still slick with oil — over her belly as I shifted up a little and slowly pushed deeper, I put my top leg over her bottom leg as I finished the fullness of my unhurried thrust.

Her body was trembling, convulsing seemingly out of control as I let my fullness rest within her.

"Oh, Blessed Spirits of the Mist!" she breathed. "You feel huge. Twice as large as your brother did."

"That is the mystery and wonder of this position," I said, kissing her shoulder. "Now relax and rest as I pleasure you, my goddess." I took her upper leg and draped it over mine, which opened her body up to me as I began slow thrusts. She responded with soft pushes of her own, pressing herself back into me. She shivered and shuddered, moaning and groaning with bliss. I slid my oiled hand up to her breasts and massaged them first one then the other, bringing each of those puckered nipples to the fullness of their own erection.

Her head turned, and, though awkward, our lips met, deep and needful. Neither of us cared that her hair was pressed between us.

Now that she was open and receptive — and the oil pushed deep — I began a faster thrust. One of her hands reached around to my butt, urging me deeper, harder. I knew she must be close to her climax. So, I slid my fingers down to her wet folds, finding her clitoris with a hard-pressing massage.

She yelped, our lips parting as her body stiffened and her eyes rolled back, mouth agape and gasping. I felt her contract around me, so tight and keen, she felt like she was milking me, urging my release.

I gasped as I felt the peak of pleasure come to me. I resisted, breathing through it, letting it fill me with pleasure, but without finishing. My cock ached, swollen and full, verging on pain, but I couldn't come yet; she hadn't commanded that of me.

Feather was fully in the throes of passion. My hand on her loins, slick with her moisture, pressed her back against me as I gave myself over to hard and insistent thrusting.

She whispered words so softly I couldn't quite hear them. When she finally gasped and spoke louder, I realized it was the same word over and over: "Pleasure, pleasure, oh... pleasure!"

I don't know how many orgasms she had, or if she just kept climbing some peak of bliss, to a more and more acute and powerful ecstasy. I lost track of time, knowing only I must continue and must not give in to the exquisite and powerful need to release.

But... I couldn't take it anymore. My cock throbbed, where agony met ecstasy. My head spun. I'd black out if I didn't...

"Please goddess," I begged. "*Please!*"

"Oh..." she gasped. "Spirits... you were... waiting for me? Yes! Please, come!"

I buried myself deep and cried out in time with her as I unleashed the full fury of my release. I came with such delicious power, it rocked me bodily; wracked with waves of tension and bliss. And she matched my ecstasy, crying out and tensing in time with me. She tightened around me again, pulling, aching, drawing out every precious drop of my climax. In the book I'd read, it had said this position could be of explosive joy for both members. The book was right.

I slid my lower arm around her, holding her tight to me;

never wanting to let her go. I wanted to remain here in this moment for eternity. And we did stay in that position, close and trembling through our mutual release until we'd melted into pools of satisfied flesh.

The candles in her room were guttering, going out, when she began to draw herself off of me. We moved, slowly and carefully, disengaging until I slid out entirely. I gasped at the cool air on my cock as she rolled, turning toward me, capturing me with a kiss of soft but intense desire.

"Thank you," she whispered. "I... I would have never... that was amazing."

"You are welcome, my goddess. Now let me leave you with a benediction." I rolled her onto her back and moved atop her for a moment. "May I forever be blessed by the goddess' lips." I kissed her lightly and felt her playful, light kisses in return. "And her neck." I kissed down over her chin to her neck. "And her glorious bosom." I probably spent a bit too much time kissing over those two large breasts, but she didn't seem to mind. "And her stomach." I kissed down over her belly. "And her loins." I tasted her, sliding my tongue through her wet folds, hearing her contented sigh. "And her legs." I kissed her thighs and calves down to her ankles, ending up scrunched on the end of her bed. "And may the goddess find serene rest, as I depart." I rose, sliding off the bed. "And in my heart, I shall pray that the goddess calls me back into her presence to worship her again someday."

Oh... wow, Agate, that was... I never had any man worship me like that. Oh yes, we'll do very well together you and I, very well indeed. Eluei seemed just as drowsy and satisfied as Feather.

Feather was squirming and drowsy again. "The goddess will let you know." Heavy-lidded eyes surveyed me. "And the goddess thanks you for your—" She eyed my cock and smiled. "—most abundant gifts this evening."

I helped her under her sheets, kissing her cheek softly as she dozed, then I dressed and left, sneaking back to Dawn's room. I knocked and Dawn answered. She wore an amused grin. "Tail left a little while ago, you certainly took your time with Feather. Did she appreciate it?"

I was fairly certain I could say: "She did."

I slipped out of Dawn's window and returned to my dorm to get what sleep I could before morning came.

CHAPTER 13

FEATHER

I WAS ROUSED BY A FORM SLIDING INTO MY BED BEHIND ME. "You're back?" I mumbled, rolling over. But it wasn't Agate who'd joined me. It was Dawn. Her Lumani was floating off in the corner of the room, a ball of fire with burning dark reds and golden oranges. The candles had gone out. Our two Lumani were the only light in the room.

"Hello," she whispered. "I was too wired to sleep. I see you're quite the opposite."

Indeed. I felt like the sands of a beach, as waves of warm contentment washed over me. Yet, there was something in the bright intensity of Dawn's golden eyes — like the rising sun — which brought me forth from my drowsy state.

I blinked... was I seeing this right? Her eyes were luminous, glowing with a faint golden light. With only the dim radiance of the two Lumani in the room it was easier to see.

"Your eyes," I breathed.

She chuckled and sighed. "Yeah, it's a Fey thing. Though, not every Fey has it, and it's usually only when we're in a state of heightened emotion."

"Fey?" I blinked coming more awake. "You're Fey... of

course you're Fey." She was the picture of Fey, even though I'd never seen one. I'd heard tell of King Alvere and Midnight, small and slight, pale skin, and dark hair.

She laughed. "Yes, one quarter Fey." She licked her lips. "I... don't like telling people of my family. Most people treat me differently once they know."

It was only then that it all came together for me. Dawn wasn't a common name in Elista but had become more common since the queen and king had named their only child. A child who had been born the same year as I had. A child who would be one-quarter Fey.

"You're... the princess," I breathed.

Oh, truly? I've always wanted to meet a Royal. Leoa was awed.

You haven't? In all your lifetimes?

I've met members of the Royal House. But in all my lives, I've never been a Noble of any true importance. I've seen kings and queens and princes and princesses, but never been this close to one. Never... been friends with one.

Oh.

Dawn grimaced. "Yup." She sighed heavily. "Does that change how you see me?"

I blinked. Did it?

At first, I thought it did. She was a princess, she was Nobility, Royalty. She was the daughter of Queen Legs! But... then I thought about it. I thought about all we'd talked about over the last day, how she'd treated me, how we'd so quickly become fast friends. She was wild and free and charismatic and powerful. She'd been all of that before I'd known who her parents were. And as much as knowing who her parents were was a revelation and might change how I saw her... it didn't change how I *felt* about her.

"No. You're just a girl who climbed into my bed to gush about the hot guys we were with, or so I'm assuming."

I felt Leoa's thrum of pleasure. *This evening was... amazing!*

Oh, yes, very much so.

Dawn grinned. "Thanks, Feather. That means a lot to me." Then, uncharacteristically, she giggled. "And wow, they were hot, weren't they?"

"So hot!" I whispered. "And experienced. Usually, I have to train the young men I'm with, but they... didn't need any instruction at all."

"How did they stack up, against all the others?" Dawn asked, bright eyed and curious. I got the sense then, that she may not be as experienced in love as me.

"Far superior to most, though..." I sighed. "I can't really compare them to my husband."

Dawn's eyes went wide. "You're married?" Her brow furrowed and she looked away, thinking. "You'd said you just got out of a..." And I saw her connect the dots. Her eyes went wide, and she looked at me. "You're... a widow?"

I nodded slowly.

"But you're only... well, you can't be older than twenty."

"I am twenty yes, the same age as you." I sighed. It was time. Here and now, in the darkness, with this strange young woman whom I hardly knew, but who was quickly becoming my closest friend, I could tell her my story. "I was married when I was eighteen."

"Spirits! Truly?"

Leoa gave a low hum. I knew she wanted to hear this as well. She said nothing, but I thought I felt... support and love from her, which warmed me and helped me go on.

I nodded. "I told you about Wilis and how he left when I was fourteen. I spent a few years after that playing with several other boys in the village, teaching them about themselves and how to love." I sighed with a breath of a laugh. "I think, thanks to me, half the boys in my village were educated in sex and women." I shook my head with a sigh. "I was... searching for something, but I didn't know what. I wanted a connection, but I was also afraid of getting too close, afraid they might leave like Wilis did. So... I left them first."

"Oh." Dawn sighed nodding. I got the sense she understood that, at least in part. She had said she didn't want anything too significant with a man right now. I was curious about what that meant, but she'd tell me in good time.

"Then..." I breathed, my heart aching, a tear coming to my eye. "Then, I saw Davas."

"You hadn't seen him before?"

I shook my head. "No, he'd just come to our village. And... he wasn't a boy."

I saw Dawn's brows rise. "A true man? Or just another one who'd matured early?"

"A true man. He was... much older."

"Oh?" Her eyes were round and large, literally gleaming with her curiosity.

Oh? Leoa echoed. I could tell she was fascinated.

"Yes, in his thirties. He'd come to our village to start a new life because he'd lost his first wife and both his children to sickness."

"That's horrible."

I nodded. "And you could see it, the depths of his love and sadness in his eyes." My throat grew tight. "It was his eyes, those caring, soulful eyes that captured my heart." For a moment I couldn't go on.

I felt Leoa's love again, seeping into me. I wondered if

this was what it would be like to be Bonded, to have that love all the time.

Yes, but I'll be much closer, stronger, more intimate. You'd feel so much more than the limited connection we have now.

"Take your time," Dawn whispered. "You don't have to say any more if you don't want to."

I shook my head, sniffing back some tears. "No, I want to, but... you're the first I've told and it's still... raw. I might need... a moment or two."

She nodded and waited patiently, as did Leoa.

I recovered after a moment, taking several deep breaths. "He wasn't looking for a new woman in his life, of course. He was a fisherman and just wanted to go out on the waters and live a quiet life. But I... I was captivated. He was so different from the boys I'd been with, which was good, but also... I didn't know how to approach him, what to say. I'd heard his story — you can't keep secrets long in a small village like ours — and I felt so sad for him. I wanted to comfort him, hold him close and heal his torn heart." I swallowed over a lump in my throat and smiled. "So, one day I hid myself under some netting on his boat before he went out. He found me once he was well out to sea and was... very surprised to see me. I still didn't know what to say, so I said the first thing that came to mind, asking him if he needed help with his fishing."

Dawn nearly choked on her guffaw and I laughed with her. Though my pain was deep, I still recalled the silly look on his face.

I got the impression of Leoa giving a sad smile, a tear on her non-existent cheek.

"'Do you know your way around a fishing boat?' he'd asked me. And I did. My father was a fisherman."

"Your father, who was actually your brother-in-law?" Dawn clarified.

"Yes." He'd been married to my sister, the woman who had raised me; whom I considered to be my mother. That made him my father.

So, I told Davas I knew a thing or two and went about helping him. We didn't say much. I had no clue what to say, and I think he was just too taken aback to say anything. It was awkward at first, but by the end of the day we were working well together. When he returned to the docks, I asked if I could help him again the next day." I sighed at the memory. "He had such an odd look on his face. I can't imagine what he was thinking: some strange girl asking to help him. He started to say 'no,' and that's... that's when I said what was in my heart." I had to pause again, overcome by emotions, tears in my eyes. I pressed my trembling lips together as I wept softly. Dawn moved in to hold me until the wave of sadness had passed. My voice was trembling when I spoke again. "I told him: 'I want to *help* you.' I saw something in his expression change as he nodded slowly. He understood then that this was about more than fishing. He took a long time, but eventually said that I could return the next day to help him. When I arrived the next morning, though... he seemed grim, walled off. He told me that I could go out with him, help with the fishing, but he wasn't interested in 'a woman.' I nodded and went with him that day, and every day after."

"And you wore him down?" Dawn asked, I could see how invested she'd become in the story.

I laughed a little at the intensity of her interest. It helped to lift my mood.

"I did, though it took almost a year. For the first month or two we hardly spoke. During the third month, I tried to start up conversations, but he would just shake his head. Then... I don't know how long later... he just started talking. At first, he talked about his previous life — before he was married — his childhood and his early family. So, I told him about mine too. Then, eventually... he told me about his wife and children. They'd been his life, and they sounded so precious and special. For a while I wondered if I could do this to him, if I wanted to try to pull him into another relationship, if I could compete with the memory of his wife and kids. But then... one miraculous day, as we were hauling in the nets together, pulling hard, we both fell back into the boat and I landed in his arms. Then, he pulled me close and held me tight and... and he cried. By the end, it was me who was holding him as he wept on my chest."

"Oh... wow."

By the Spirits, Leoa whispered.

"And when he was done, he looked up at me and finally asked me why I was there with him. I told him then, as I looked into those sad gray eyes of his, that I loved him. That I felt like I'd always loved him, that my soul was made for his and I wanted to soothe his pain and heal his heart and... and... well, I didn't get much further than that because he was kissing me."

I rolled onto my back, looking up at the dark contours of my small room. "We were married in the fall. I had just turned eighteen. We had two glorious years together." Things were getting harder and harder to say. I swallowed over the growing lump in my throat and sniffed back tears. "I... I miscarried once."

"Oh, Feather, that's awful!"

My dear, I have suffered that pain and feel so deeply for you, Leoa soothed.

It had been. I'd been devastated and had leaned on him

then, enfolding myself in his love for me. "But it was probably for the best, or I'd have a child now and I'd never had gone for the Choosing and met you..." I said with another sniffle. The pain, from the loss of a child I'd never known, could never completely be assuaged, but the love of friendship I felt from Dawn did wonders for my aching heart.

"I am glad we met," Dawn said softly. She was rubbing my shoulder. I knew she wouldn't ask... ask how Davas died. I'd have to say that on my own.

"This past winter, Davas got the Dream Fever. We sent for a healer, but they didn't get there in time. He lay abed for two days, then... he was gone." My voice was barely there, so choked up with emotions.

I'm so sorry, Feather. Leoa sent more love and warmth.

Dawn squirmed a little closer and held me again, slipping an arm under my head to pull me close to her bosom. She was in a sleeping shift, and I stained the silk with my tears. I had already cried for weeks about this, and had thought myself past the worst of it, but there was still such a gaping hole in my soul where Davas had been. I still loved him so much and wanted him back, but I knew that wasn't happening. And for now, I didn't want to love a man, not like I'd loved Davas. I would play and let them sooth me, comfort me, please me, but nothing more. I wasn't ready yet. I didn't even know when I would be.

I woke with a start, surprised I'd fallen asleep on Dawn's chest.

"I think you wore yourself out," she said softly, stroking my hair. "Thank you for telling me of Davas. I know that couldn't have been easy." I felt her soft kiss on the top of my head. "I know now, we're going to be the closest of friends you and me." That warmed me immensely. "Rest, Feather," she said, and I closed my eyes again, feeling far more at peace than I had in a long, long time.

She was still there when I woke the next morning.

"We're going to skip our classes today," she said softly, sounding a bit worn out herself. Had she been awake all night? "Instead, we're going to do something fun."

CHAPTER 14

DAWN

FEY COULD LAST FOR A FEW DAYS WITHOUT SLEEP. I WAS ONLY part Fey, so I was just a little drained as the sun rose. Still, I was excited. I knew my new friend needed a break, something wonderous and fulfilling. She'd shared something special with me last night, so I'd share something special with her today.

We were going to the Mists.

We dressed and went to breakfast, making sure to steal some extra bits of food, which we packed away for our lunch. Then, when the gates were opened for the day, we skipped out on our lessons and hurried out into the countryside around Silverveil.

I don't think I've ever known a human so intent on breaking convention and throwing off the rules. Amya wasn't scorning or rebuking, just commenting with a bit of awe in his voice.

Isn't it wonderful? I said, turning my face up to the spring sun as Feather and I walked over the hills around Silverveil.

There is a freedom to this. I fear for consequences though.

I shrugged. *They may come, and I'll take them if they do. But in truth, everything I'm doing is to Bond with you, and since that's what I'm supposed to be doing here, I can't see how it's that bad.*

And Feather? Is this what she needs to Bond?

Rule-breaking? Probably not, but I guarantee you, that our trip today will help.

To the Mists?

Yes, you know the way, right?

I do.

And it's something every Silverveil student does eventually. I'm just going early. I know it will help Feather.

True. Amya sounded just a bit skeptical. Then he sighed. *I know your intentions are good, but... be careful young one. Your lust for adventure and freedom may someday hurt this friend of yours. You need to consider what she needs as well.*

That... was probably true, but today I *was* considering what she needed. A trip into the Mists would help us both.

"I can't believe I'm going to see the Mists!" Feather said, more than usually filled with exuberance and life. Her Lumani, in the shape of some small rodent, was also bouncing excitedly on her shoulder. I shook my head again. Feather had already chosen a shape. She was like my mother, who'd chosen her spider form upon arrival at Silverveil. I apparently would take a little longer.

Perhaps the Mists will help? Amya said.

Perhaps.

I drank in a long breath of the cool spring-morning air. "I know, isn't this just a wonderful day?" I chuckled a little. "After a wonderful night."

Feather gave a throaty laugh. "Oh, yes indeed. So, tell me, what did you think of the two brothers?"

My mind wandered back to the two very different encounters. Agate had been curious and exciting, stimu-lating because of the newness and even the awkwardness of the experience. A shudder ran through me as I relived it in my mind. Yes, that had been... something new... and wonderful.

Tail... had been so very different, though. I'd expected a similar sort of desire for the extreme, but instead he'd been attentive, caring, seeking only what I wished and needed and providing that. It had been a more sedate session, but no less stimulating for its solemnity. He'd kissed me all over, and with my skin already being roused and responsive that had been a wonderful sensation. Then we'd lain, kissing softly and deeply as he'd worked magic with his fingers to stoke my passion once again. Yet even then, though I was riding high on waves of bliss, he'd taken his time, remaining beside me, entering me and beginning with slow, sensual movements. It drove me crazy and piled on my pleasure in ever increasing heaps as he steadily built up his pace and passion. Then, with my entire being burning for him, I'd taken control, rolling us, straddling him and riding him hard to further peaks of bliss. And he had used his strong hands to good measure, caressing me as I ground upon him. And when he finally, exquisitely, found his release, I'd joined him in a mutual moment of ecstasy. I'd never felt so powerful before, so in control. I'd been shown the position by the man I'd purchased in Weijin but had not known it's true power and bliss until last night.

Feather laughed. "Lost in remembrances, are you?"

I'd forgotten she'd asked about the brothers which had prompted my blissful reminiscence. I laughed. "Ah... yeah, sorry."

"So, a good experience, then?" Something in how she said that suggested she knew I hadn't had many 'experiences.' She wasn't wrong.

"Oh, very much so. Agate was experimental and innovative and quirky. It was curious and wonderous and very... stimulating."

Feather laughed. "Yes, he tried something new with me too." Given how experienced she was, I found that curious. "What about Tail?"

"He was attentive and caring and just... so... *there* for me. He made sure I had everything I needed... multiple times, before he found his pleasure." I reconsidered that. "No, that's not right. As much as he peaked at the end, the whole time he seemed to take pleasure in my pleasure."

Feather nodded. "That pretty much sums them up for me as well."

"And... would you want to have another go with them?" I asked. I did, very much, hopefully soon.

Feather hedged a little. "Yes, probably. I actually did suggest it to them both."

"But...?" I prompted.

She sighed. "I told you about... about Davas last night. I really don't want to get too attached to another man right now. And given how... full of affection those two were, I fear I could start to fall for them."

"Ah." I nodded. "I'll just have them both then."

Feather gave me a sidelong look with a faint grin. "Together?"

That would be new. And suddenly I very much wanted to try that. I'd have to ask if they'd be interested... well, I probably didn't have to ask. They'd be interested.

"Is there anyone else you've had your eye on?" I asked, curious. Neither of us had been here that long, but perhaps she'd seen someone she liked.

She giggled just a little and it reminded me how cheerful and ebullient she was, how refreshing and full of life. "Well..."

"Really, already?"

"I'm sure you've seen him too, the big guy."

The big guy? As if there were only one. Everyone was bigger than me. So, I asked: "Big guy?"

"The one with the baby face and big green eyes."

Nope, I hadn't noticed him at all.

I have, Amya said softly. *He is indeed big, a head taller than any other man here and very noticeable. I'm surprised you haven't seen him.*

I'm small, everyone else gets in my way.

Ah... yes, true.

"Do you know his name?" I asked.

"No, but I think Agate knows him, I think they're in the same group."

"That could be awkward, asking a former lover for the name of your next lover."

"True." She nodded. "I'll find a way."

I was sure she would. I sighed. "I'm... I'm very thankful you opened up to me about... your marriage," I said gently. "That meant a lot to me. I... I've never had a true, close friend." That wasn't true. I'd had Eadric for years now, but this was so very different. I corrected myself: "A *girl* friend. Is that... how you think of me?" I was a bit hesitant. I hoped I knew the answer but didn't want to presume.

Feather grinned. "Of course! I've only known you for a day, but we've become fast friends, Dawn." She reached down and clasped my hand in hers, squeezing it for a moment before releasing me.

That warmed my heart. It felt good to have someone like this. Someone I could be close to with no expectations of sex or anything like that. Just... friends.

You've done so much, yet been so sheltered, Amya said softly, comforting.

I smiled. It was true, but now, things were changing.

Feather seemed a bit tentative when she asked. "You once said you weren't really interested in a significant relationship right now... is... there a story behind that?"

Ah... yes.

Is there? Amya said.

There is, sort of, yes.

"I... just... don't want to be tied down right now, I want to be free."

Feather nodded. "Was your childhood restricted, growing up as a princess?"

I marveled at her insight. "Restricted is putting it kindly." But that wasn't all of it. "I had tutors and teachers and every hour of every day was structured. Even my 'play time' was set and limited." I felt tension creeping into my shoulders and rolled them to try to release it. I didn't much like thinking about my childhood. "But... there was... more." I felt some of my building tension slip away when I laughed. "You have your hard tale, and I have mine, though... I don't think mine's nearly as rough as yours." I sighed. "I haven't suffered the loss you have. In fact, I've always had everything. And that... was part of the problem."

"Oh?" She sounded truly curious.

I was sure I'd distance us by telling her this, that she'd not understand why I felt the way I did about my upbringing.

No, don't dictate what she thinks. You won't know that until you tell her. It may be as you suspect or it may not, either way, the telling will only serve to get it out into the open to be dealt with.

Wise words. I supposed that was to be expected from one who'd lived several lifetimes already.

"I had everything... except love," I said softly.

I let that hang for a while and Feather eventually responded with, "What about your parents?"

I nodded. "I'm sure they loved me, in their way, but they had an odd way of showing it. They were the king and queen, of two countries. They had a lot on their plate and often did not have time for me. I spent a lot of time with their surrogates, my 'family' was a bit odd. In truth I had three fathers and two mothers. And often I was with one of the others, not my true parents. Or I'd be with one parent and one of the others. It was rare I was alone with just my mother and father."

Feather nodded. "I suppose they must have been busy. I can't imagine what it's like to run two nations."

Exactly.

"So, I knew they loved me... in my mind, but in my heart, I felt... well, they felt distant. And that, combined with my lack of freedom, meant I felt just a little stifled and pushed away from them." I sighed heavily. "So, when I was sent to live with the Fey, with my Ona Ahmaia — my grandmother on my father's side — for three years, I felt like I'd been set free... initially. But even though the Fey live a mostly limitless existence, I was still... busy all the time. It was different, but after a while it felt like just another prison of people who loved me, but in a distant way. The Fey are... very restrained in showing emotion." Though... Eadric hadn't been distant when he'd finally admitted how he felt... it had just taken him five years to get there.

"So, when I was to return to my parents, I escaped my guards and ran away. I was capable enough and could take care of myself. And I had a sort-of friend, a male friend, with me to join in my adventures."

"Truly? You haven't mentioned anyone until now? How long were you together?"

"Well, that's the question... we were with each other for five years, but we were never really... *together*, if you get my meaning. We were near but not *close*. I didn't want to be. He did, but I pushed him away."

"But after all that time with everyone being distant, didn't you want someone to love you?"

A simple question, posed so clearly and... I didn't know how to answer it.

CHAPTER 15

DAWN

I SHOULD HAVE WANTED SOMEONE TO LOVE ME, SHOULDN'T I? So then... why had I pushed Eadric away? I thought I knew. "I... he was very intense in his affections. So as much as he loved me, I felt... trapped again." Yet something about that didn't ring true, not with how Feather had so clearly stated things.

"Ah," Feather said, seemingly understanding. "He wouldn't let you be free, which is all you really wanted."

That made sense, though... some part of me still questioned why I hadn't accepted such love when it had been offered to me. I could have set rules, told him what I needed, but I hadn't. I'd just kept him at arm's length. There was a niggling feeling there, which I didn't want to think about now. I pushed it down and went on.

"So, I saw the world and all its wonders." This part made me happy. I smiled as I recalled my many adventures. "The Dhar'me mystics of Isharu, the Burning Lands and Fire Wyrms. The Okuri, who learned to breathe fire from the original dragons. Intelligent animals that could speak, and men who spoke to the dead. A nation that lived in the mountains and had ships that flew between ports. The Weijin Sea Singers and Earth Dancers. And an entire nation where women ruled and men served. Can you imagine that?"

"Most of what you just said seems beyond imagining," Feather said, shaking her head, eyes wide. "The world truly is an amazing place."

"It is, and... I never would have seen it if I hadn't taken my life into my own hands and done as I wished."

"Like you're doing today?"

I let out a free and hearty laugh. "Exactly. Though I also thought you deserved to see the wonders of the Mists. It seems like you've seen so much sorrow in your life. I wanted to give you something... amazing."

"What're the Mists like?" she asked.

I laughed again. "No clue, I've never been there, your Lumani could probably tell you. I'm looking forward to this too." I quickly added: "But, just because I've never seen them doesn't mean I don't know that the Mists are amazing."

"I've only heard about them in faerie-tales. I lived at the other end of Elista. Few from my village have ever been this far from home."

"So, this is all a grand adventure for you?" I liked that thought.

She gave a nervous laugh. "Yes, but I'm terrified half the time, where you seem so... excited and... confident."

I reached over to grasp her hand and hold it in both of mine, walking sideways for a moment. "Feather, I'm not without fear. There were many times in my travels when I was afraid. But I've also learned that... I am capable. I can deal with nearly anything. And I know you have that strength inside you, too."

"How did you deal with those things you feared?" she asked softly.

I released one of my hands on hers to walk normally beside her again, her hand still clasped in mine. "I feared not understanding people, so I learned bits of their language. I've always been quick to pick up languages, and I think most of the southern continent must have come from one or two original peoples long ago, as there were many similarities in their languages. Once I knew one well enough, I could muddle through that of their neighbors until I understood it better. So... I talked my way out of a lot of troubles. And when talking didn't work... Well, sometimes I fought, sometimes I ran."

"You know how to fight?"

I did indeed. "I was trained in hand-fighting by Midnight as a child. Then, with the Fey I learned how to use my cloth abilities and studied their own unique art of combat."

"Could you... teach me?"

"Of course," I said with a squeeze of her hand.

"If I'm going to Bond and... well, I have no clue what will happen after that, but I know that True-Bonded are the leaders and protectors of Elista. I should learn how to defend myself at least."

"And I'll teach you. Also, I know exactly what you're going to do once you're Bonded."

She laughed. "You do? Tell me."

"You're going to join the new Noble House I'm going to start."

Feather looked at me, one brow raised. "You're going to start a Noble House? That sounds ambitious." She laughed again. "Though, knowing you, I shouldn't be surprised. I'm assuming you've worked it all out?"

"Mostly," I said nodding. "I didn't know who my second was going to be until I met you, but now I do. We'll steal away all the promising new Nobles from this crop of Silver-veil, then start a House where rules are... optional."

"And do you think the queen — your mother — will allow that?"

"She won't have a say in it. I'll start it no matter what. I don't care if it's on the official lists or not. If they don't want to recognize our House, that's their loss."

Feather just shook her head for a long moment. "I don't think I could ever be as daring as you are."

"I'll teach you that too," I said softly, smiling. Then I drew in a long breath. "You want to learn to fight? Let's start with something simple, something we can practice as we walk."

She looked at me, brows raised. "Oh?"

"Yes, how you move, how you walk, can make the difference between being caught off guard and avoiding a surprise attack. You need to be light on your feet, agile, smooth."

"Is that why you're so graceful when you move?"

I'd never thought of myself as graceful, but... "I suppose so."

Feather drew in a breath, smiling. "Then show me, please. I'd love to have your grace and poise."

I took that compliment with a smile and nodded, releasing her hand to walk freely beside her. "Here's how to start. First, stand straight, butt in, stomach in, shoulders down and back, and head high. It may help to imagine there is a rope attached to the top of your head and it's pulling you up." I demonstrated, even going so far as to lift onto my toes as I walked.

I watched Feather out of the corner of my eye as she

followed my instructions, though for her, one of the results was a rather dramatic thrusting out of her already significant chest. Spirits, if she mastered this, no man would be able to resist her, tall and proud and leading with those magnificent tits! Though, that gave me a thought. I wasn't top-heavy like her. "You may need to lean back just a touch, to distribute your weight evenly in a line down your body over your feet, you're... ah..."

"A little heavy in front? Yeah, I know."

She looked awkward for a long moment as she stretched up and leaned back a little, walking on her toes to match me.

"This feels so strange," she said.

"It probably will for a while, until you get used to it. And, this is only part one of the walk."

"Oh? There's more? This seems challenging enough."

"If it helps, don't keep walking on your toes, but keep leading with your toes. Let them hit the ground first. Keep your weight on the toes and front of the foot, keep the heel light, barely touching the ground. That's it... toe-heel, toe-heel."

I demonstrated, settling down a little, and Feather followed. "Oh, that is easier yes."

"Now, keeping yourself still straight and poised, through the upper body, sink down just a little through the legs, let them bend and absorb all your weight as you move, keep yourself steady through each transition of the legs, weight and balance even."

I watched her as she did as I'd demonstrated. She picked it up quickly, moving through each step and transition with balance and poise.

"I'm going to try to push you over, just keep walking if you can."

"I'll try."

I started low, pushing gently on her hips. They swayed out to the side and she swayed with them, but she kept her balance. I pushed on her side and she swayed a bit more, needing to take a step to one side, but she kept on walking. Finally, I reached up to push on her shoulder, putting a bit more strength into it. And as I'd hoped, her upper body bent and she had to take a step to correct and catch herself, but she did it and stayed on her feet.

"Can you feel how free and light you are?" I asked.

She nodded. "Yes, it's still awkward, but... I feel... stronger, surer."

"Keep practicing it, and you'll get used to it. This walk makes you lighter on your feet while at the same time, sinking you powerfully into the ground. You'll be hard to knock off balance and better able to react to anything around you." I pushed her suddenly, with a good portion of my not inconsiderable strength, low on the hips.

She bent and stumbled but didn't fall.

"See?"

She laughed. "Indeed. I... wasn't expecting that, but I was still able to catch myself."

"Exactly. You can vary your stride a little, but shorter strides will allow you to keep your weight evenly distributed as you move." I nodded. "You're doing really well: graceful and poised and walking like a dancer."

She smiled.

We walked in silence for a long moment, as she concentrated on her walk. Then she asked. "You mentioned something about cloth abilities? What's that?"

"It's a Fey thing. All Fey have an affinity to some part of nature. Some to earth, some to metal, some to water, some to wood and some to other plants. Since most clothes come from plants, that means some of us can manipulate cloth. We can't work with wool, silk, or other cloth that comes from animals, but cotton, linen, hemp, and jute we can work with." To demonstrate, I made a twirling upward motion with my hand and made the skirt of her dress flare up and out a little.

"Oh!" she said with a pleasant surprise.

"It's a mostly harmless ability, but it can be used to constrict limbs, choke people with their own collars, or even make them move as you wish, like a marionette, though I haven't mastered that. My ability is a bit diluted, being only a quarter Fey." Still, I felt like showing off. "Want to see something fun I can do though?"

Feather nodded with an eager look.

I had to stop; I couldn't do it while walking. I gathered all my control with cloth and gently made my pants and shirt press in on me, not constricting, but holding me firmly, then... I lifted the cloth and floated up off the ground. It took all my concentration and drained my strength considerably to do even this. I couldn't get much higher than a foot or so, but still, I was effectively flying.

"Oh! Dawn, that's amazing!" Feather breathed.

I set myself down and released the cloth with a heavy huff of a breath, trying not to show how much that had drained me.

"You can fly!" Feather said, still marveling. The wonder on her face, the sheer open joy and innocence, made me smile. "I've always wanted to fly. To be—" She laughed. "Well to be as light as a feather and dance around the skies."

"I can't quite do that, mostly I just float a little," I admitted.

"Still, it must be wonderful."

Her expression of wonder was a bit contagious, and I

beamed back at her. I nodded. It was amazing how Feather brought out the joy I seemed to have suppressed in myself. Things I could do, which were just... normal and part of me... were a wonder to her, and that made me realize, just a bit, how special I was.

"Thank you, Feather," I said softly, taking her hand again as we continued walking, giving it a squeeze. "Thank you, so much."

"For what?" she asked, confused.

"Just... being you."

She laughed. "Oh... Anytime."

We walked for a while in peace after that. Two new friends, bonding simply by being close and enjoying a beautiful day together.

We reached the Mists just after noon. The walk to the Mists took longer than it did in my mother's day. Scholars had determined the Mists were drifting southeast at a rate of roughly a fifth of a mile a year, which took them away from Silverveil. I considered telling Feather about the story behind that, but that was my mother's story, not mine. And when the Mists came into view, I forgot all of that.

Feather and I stood, stunned, watching the slow, swirling dance of heavy fog.

I felt their pull, their power. "Can you feel that?" I said, awed.

"Yes," she said, voice soft and breathy. "It's calling to me."

Be careful, young one. Do not become too enamored of the call of the Mists, for that is how Mistweavers are made. You must remain yourself, who you are in your heart, at all times while in the Mists, but also... submit to them and their power. Be yourself, allow them to affect you, but do not... succumb to their power. Amya was insistent.

"Is your Lumani telling you what to do?" I asked softly.

"Yes," Feather breathed again. "Remain strong: submit, but do not give in."

Are you ready? Amya asked.

Suddenly I didn't know. I drew in a long breath and centered myself. *Yes.*

Then step inside.

Feather and I moved together, cautious and careful, until the Mists devoured us and though she had been next to me, I could see Feather no longer.

"Feather?" I called, and there was no response.

I was alone... well, except for Amya, still floating next to me.

I felt a chill shiver down my spine.

Remain strong, Amya warned. I took another breath to regain myself.

What happens if I don't remain strong? I asked.

You could lose yourself here... forever.

CHAPTER 16

FEATHER

I was more than a little scared as I stepped into the swirling gray wall and the Mists enveloped me.

Fear is not a bad thing, Feather, Leoa said softly. Her small rodent form had lifted off from my shoulder once we were in the Mists and floated around me like she had when she was a ball of energy. It was strange to watch the small, mousy form 'swimming' through the Mists. *Fear protects us from danger, and there are dangers in the Mists.*

But...? I asked, hoping there was a 'but.'

Leoa gave a soft chuckle. *Yes, as you suspect, there is a 'but.'* I felt her drawing a heavy breath. *But fear limits us. It reduces you to a baser being, an animal, where your options are only to fight or flee or freeze. You must learn to tame your fear. To feel it, but not to let it control you.*

How do I do that?

By knowing you're more powerful than any foe you might face.

I am?

Here in the Mists you are, yes. There are beings that might drain you of energy completely by accident, but I'll keep them away from you. They don't even see you as you. It's like you're a flower they might pick. And everything else here is of a different world so removed from yours that they wouldn't even know how to harm you. In truth, the only thing here that can hurt you... is you.

Me?

Another soft laugh. Yes. In the Mists, things are as you make them. There is no ground beneath you unless you believe there to be. The trees you see are not there. You can walk right through them... Unless you wish them to be real and firm, then they are. I have heard of Chosen who trip over... nothing... in the Mists, then fall, expecting something hard or sharp to hit them... and so it does, and it wounds or kills them. But if you can control your fear here, then this is a world of wonders. You can fly, or fall for an eternity, you can imagine the kiss of a lover and feel it on your lips.

That last thought was intriguing. I did want to fly, but first perhaps I'd try something simpler. I closed my eyes and imagined Tail next to me. Suddenly I felt his warmth, his hard body close. I imagined him cupping my face and kissing me, and I felt his hands and the soft brush of his lips. I lost myself in that fantasy for a moment, feeling one of his hands smooth the dress down over my form, pressing to my every curve. Then he was pulling up my dress, warm hand on my thigh and caressing inward.

I shuddered at his ephemeral touch and blinked my eyes open to see... nothing but Mists. His touch vanished, leaving me just a little hot.

"Oh!" I breathed heavily.

Leoa Laughed. That's a first. I don't think I've known anyone who's made out with the Mists quite that sensuously before. But yes, the Mists can be your lover, if that is what you wish. They can be anything.

I imagined the strong hands of a large man easily lifting me off the ground. The forest floor, which I could barely see at my feet, lifted away and vanished.

Am I flying?

It would seem so, yes. But try it without the imagined hands. Just... let yourself be free and fly!

I wasn't sure I was ready for that just yet. Instead, I imagined myself becoming my current namesake, a feather in the palm of the man holding me. And... I felt like I was shrinking or that imagined man growing to impossible heights. And indeed, I was a feather, I was light and the Mists moved through my weightless vanes. I imagined a light breeze which lifted me and I floated free, tossed higher and higher. A thrill, unlike anything I'd ever felt, filled me.

I'm flying!

Isn't it wonderful? Leoa said with glee. *You're good at this. Keep it up, what else do you want from the Mists?*

I want to meet more like you, like your kind, I want to see and feel the Spirits! And suddenly the Mists were no longer gray, but a living world of every possible color. I gasped at the wonder revealed before me. Bright balls in every possible color floated, some still, some bobbing by slowly, others whipping about with great speed. Other beings or... something... like long streamers in shimmering shades of shifting color sailed by slowly, some distant, some near, but all seeming — oddly — the same size. The perspective was all wrong. The distant ones would have to be huge to appear as they did.

Then suddenly one was before me and it was huge.

Oh Feather, watch out! A flare of pale pinks and blues pushed me away from the being. I watched the shifting, shimmering rainbow that was the large beast sail past me at a safe distance.

Thanks, I said, turning to Leoa, and upon seeing her all words left me. She was... so incredibly beautiful! She was semi-human with a torso and head, but below her waist was feathery tendrils, like a shifting skirt. Her arms were similar, stretching out long and fading away to either side. Her face was too smooth, her nose a little softened and flat, her mouth wide, eyes far too large and glowing with a bright internal light.

"Leoa!" I breathed.

She smiled and cocked her head to one side. "Few have seen me like this." Her voice was radiant yet soft. And it was a voice, it was outside of me, not in my head.

Leoa laughed, a sound like tinkling chimes. "This is how I see myself in the Mists now, after having been a part of humans for so long."

She drew close. "You must be very careful here, in this vision," she said softly, embracing me in her glowing warmth. "That Bog'haral you summoned could have swum right through you and consumed you. Everything here is beautiful, but some, as I said, are dangerous."

Oddly, now, I wasn't afraid at all. "How could things so beautiful be dangerous?" I breathed.

Leoa laughed. "Many beautiful things are dangerous. You are beautiful and when we are Bonded, you will have greater power. You might become dangerous. And certainly, Dawn has a... dangerous side to her, and you believe her to be beautiful."

That was true.

"Is there a spirit I can meet, a safe one?"

Leoa nodded. "Yes." She reached out with one of her impossibly long waving 'arms' and seemed to snag a small ball of yellow light. "Feather, meet a Sprite. Hold out your hand, be gentle." I did as asked, and Leoa set the light into my cupped hands. The light intensified for a moment before becoming a tiny little woman, no taller than the width of my finger. She possessed gossamer wings, which were three or four times the size of her body, stretching out far behind her. She took a graceful step then began flitting over my palm. I felt the press of her fine feet as she waved and swayed in a most beautiful dance.

"Oh!" My heart swelled as I absorbed the intensity of passion and beauty from this Sprite. "She's so beautiful and..." I didn't have the words to describe her.

Leoa laughed again. "Odd you should say that. Sprites have no true form other than light and energy... but they can be seen as a reflection of the beholder. You are seeing the purest expression of yourself."

"Oh..." My eyes widened. I swallowed hard and felt a tear at my eye.

"Exactly. And if you're curious, this is how I see you too."

I had no words again. Emotions swelled up to claim me and I wept free and joyous tears. Never before had I felt so connected with myself; my beauty and power.

"Thank you," I finally managed to say. "Thank you so much for this precious gift."

The sprite lifted from my palm and danced away as golden light once more. Leoa embraced me, holding me close. "You are most welcome, for you are a precious gift to me as well. Through you I will grow and experience more of the world. I am glad I could help you grow and experience my world as well."

"Your world is amazing," I breathed.

"I cannot say for certain, but I think you are the first human to have seen it. At least, the first human I've Bonded with."

"I feel... so... connected with... everything," I said softly.

Drawing a long breath, I felt more alive than ever before. I put a hand to my chest and closed my eyes, so full of emotions I felt tears well and release.

"This is your gift, I think," Leoa said. "Your connection, your compassion, your love. I am glad I could help you delve deeper into it. I think if you continue to explore this, we will soon be Bonded."

I nodded. "Thank you," I whispered, emotions thick in my voice. I opened my eyes to the wonders of this place and simply gazed upon them. Leoa was there, next to me, holding me close, safe from harm. And so we stayed for some time, before I finally knew I must leave the Mists, for if I didn't, I might never leave this place of astounding beauty.

Leoa returned to her rodent form as I imagined returning to the Mists. The vision of the spirits faded until I was once again surrounded by gray fog. Leoa told me to imagine stepping out of the Mists, and I did. Once I was safely back into the forest, I fell to my knees and wept, tears of joy and wonder at my incredible supernatural experience.

CHAPTER 17

DAWN

THE TREES WERE LIKE GRASSES, TINY AND BARELY VISIBLE through the Mists at my feet. With the brush of a toe, I could knock over a towering pine. I'd never felt so powerful.

When Amya had told me to experiment with the Mists, the first thing I'd thought of was how I'd always been small. I wanted to be huge... and so I was.

You're certain I won't accidentally step on Feather? I asked, just a bit worried for the other woman, my new friend.

You won't, she is far removed from this place now, experiencing her own wonders. She is safe, you can tromp around to your heart's content.

I won't even hurt the trees?

The trees you see are of the Mists, they will restore themselves if crushed. It is the way of all things here, life and restoration.

If you say so. I lifted my giant foot and stomped down hard, feeling the shudder of the earth. It was... satisfying. So... I did it again, beginning to run through the Mists as a giant.

Is this truly what it takes to make you feel strong? Amya asked, still bobbing along next to me, oddly they hadn't shrunk as I'd grown, they were the same size they'd always been in comparison to me.

I stopped and sighed. I knew this was petty. And yet... *I've always been... small, smaller than everyone else, except young children and a few Fey. I know that I'm strong, I just... wanted to experience what it would be like to be... big.*

I felt myself retracting, shrinking and once again the trees — the ones I could see through the thick, billowing fog — towered above me.

I leaned against a tree and nearly fell over when it wasn't actually there to support me. I recalled, only then, my mother's tale of her experience in the Mists, how she'd put her hand through a tree and marveled at how it wasn't really there. What else had she experienced? Flying and falling and how she'd realized the Mists weren't really mist at all.

I closed my eyes and focused, centering myself. I simply... *felt* everything around me, and in that moment. I felt the cold — but so very dry — brush of the Mists upon my skin.

What is it you have come to the Mists seeking? Amya asked, voice soft within me, curious.

Truth. I replied before I even really knew what I was saying.

Ah, very wise. There are... many truths in the Mists. Is there one among the many you seek?

I want to know... my truth, I said and felt a tremor run through me. I wasn't sure where these words were coming from. I'd never been one for deep introspection before.

Ah, yes, then give yourself over to the Mists. Again, remain strong, but submit. Do not lose yourself, but simply... seek the wisdom of the Mists.

This all seemed just a little paradoxical to me: be strong

but submit, give yourself, but don't lose yourself. How was I to do that?

Even before I could ask, Amya guided me. *You are already doing it. Continue to just... feel the Mists. But next allow them beyond the barrier of your skin. Allow the Mists to seek the truths within you and show them to you. But... while doing so, keep your heart strong and sure.*

I let myself go, just a little, feeling deeper into the Mists, while allowing them to feel deeper into me. And suddenly it all made sense, not my truths, not yet, but how to interact with the Mists. It was a give and take. You allowed them in while diving into them as well.

Mistweavers allow the Mists in, but do not seek through the Mists in return. They are overtaken by the Mists. I didn't even make it a question I just... knew.

Yes. They seek its power because they do not believe in the power they already possess. They give themselves too much to the Mists and as such the power of the Mists corrupts them. The human mind and soul were not meant to take on the power of the Mists. But... oddly, they can... share it. When you are as strong as the Mists you are understanding your own power.

This much I understood now. For as I let the Mists *inside* me, I was also seeking deeper and deeper into the Mists themselves.

What is my truth? I asked softly.

Amya knew I wasn't speaking to him.

The answer did not come immediately, and it didn't come in words. It came... in movement. I felt myself begin to sway and didn't know why, until I felt the Mists themselves moving within and around me. I was moving them, and they were moving me and... through this movement came an understanding. I could suddenly *feel* out through the Mists themselves in an almost physical manner. I felt the hard, rough bark of the trees and also felt inside them to the fibrous fluids that kept them alive and growing. I felt... life, animals, the brush of fur and the heat of breath. I even felt the odd and ephemeral beings that lived in the Mists. With fingers of Mist, I held them, feeling their power, their light, their energy. They were weightless and yet heavy with presence and potential all at once... like... me. I was small and — as Feather liked to note — weightless in my movements, but I'd also often been told of the puissant aura I gave off.

I laughed. *I'm like the beings of the Mists,* I said softly. *Weightless but weighty, powerful but ephemeral, small but with a massive soul.*

And is that your truth? Amya asked.

It was... a part of it... but there was more. I went back to swaying with the Mists again, moving a shoulder back and out of the way of... something, some being of the Mists.

That was impressive. How did you know that Wisp was there? They are so small even us Lumani have trouble remembering they're there some days.

I... just knew. I felt it. I can feel so much here. I... just... know how everything is connected. Even the tiniest movements cause so many ripples in the Mist.

Ah, yes, true.

Connection, I breathed the word and knew it was so very right in that moment. *Connection is my truth. Not so much being connected to all things, but... feeling how everything is connected. Sensing the intricacies of being and movement and life and knowing what it means. I... think — no, I know — that is my truth!*

Amazing, yes, I can feel it too. Good for you Dawn!

I let myself float in this place of knowing for a while longer, feeling the movement of everything around me, from the brush of a breeze upon the tiniest blade of grass to the massive sweep of some large spirit high above me in the Mists. I could feel it all. It was a massive, complex dance and I was a part of it. And when I swayed and flowed with it, I felt so in tune with myself and my being.

I laughed at the freedom I felt. Yes. This was true freedom, letting yourself go and moving with the existence of all things.

But then... my mind caught on a snag of a thought. *If I was meant to move with all things, then... does that mean I must follow the rules?*

I didn't know I'd spoken those words until Amya answered them. *No, I do not think so. The movement you are feeling is far beyond the rules of men. You are connecting with the chaos of nature. There are some rules to this expansive dance, but they are not rules which can be broken anyway. I believe, your nature is to move to this universal dance, follow it and its chaos and ignore the rules of your world. That... would be truly radical would it not?*

It would, yes. I was so very thankful for Amya's wisdom. *I wish I could hug you,* I said softly. *You have been such an... amazing teacher and friend and...* I didn't know what else to say.

Use your gift, feel me as I truly am, and you shall feel my warmth.

In my place of union with all things I reached out and pulled Amya close, feeling the intensity of spirit and the comforting warmth of their presence. He enveloped me and I enveloped him and, for a moment, we were joined in a far more intimate way than any lover.

You have... so much love to give, I whispered. I could feel it.

As do you, my child. And through you, I shall express all my love. Together we shall know no bounds.

I would have thought we'd have Bonded in that moment,

but alas, we simply remained spiritually embracing each other for a long time. There was no more than that.

I sighed.

I think perhaps I should return. I didn't know how long I'd been in the Mists but it felt like an eternity. *Feather may be waiting.*

Indeed, she is, Amya said softly. *I... feel blessed to have shared this moment with you, Dawn. I know we shall Bond, soon.* Amya laughed faintly. *Just keep being... radical.*

I will.

I knew I only had to think of leaving the Mists and I would. So, I slowly extracted myself from all of what I was feeling, releasing the Mists from myself as well, then walked out of that magical place.

Feather was sitting, leaning against a tree nearby. She looked so serene and peaceful. Then one of her beatific smiles spread onto her face, upon seeing me.

"How was it?" she asked.

There was only one word to describe it. "Magical," I said. And I could see in her sable-brown eyes, that it had been the same for her.

"Oh!" she breathed. "Your Lumani!"

I looked at Amya, but he wasn't a glowing ball anymore, instead he was a small rodent with a long tail and long back legs. I blinked. I'd seen that before. Hurrying over to Feather I let Amya down into my hands as she did the same with her Lumani.

And indeed, except for the colors which swirled around their semi-ethereal forms, they were identical.

We'd both Bonded with the same animal avatar.

CHAPTER 18

FEATHER

WE ATE OUR LUNCH UNDER THE SHADE OF THE TREES NEXT TO the swirling Mists. We told each other of our experiences and marveled over our identical avatars. It wasn't unheard of for two True-Bonded to have a similar avatar, two similar breeds of dogs, or very similar types of insects, but identical avatars? I'd never heard of such a thing, and neither had Dawn. And from Leoa's reaction, neither had she. We knew then, our friendship must be fated.

We assumed it had something to do with our similar purpose. The Mists had revealed to both of us, a need for *connection*. I felt like I was meant to connect emotionally with people. Dawn felt like she was meant to *feel* the connection between all things. Our purposes were similar, but subtly different.

We walked slowly back to Silverveil in the afternoon, arriving as evening fell. Master Crab scolded us for leaving, but... I was feeling more and more like Dawn was right. If we were going to Bond, it would be in our own ways. So, Dawn had a long and painstaking conversation with Master Crab, explaining that we needed freedom to find our Bond and he, in his own, incoherent way, nodded and told us to "do what felt right." After that we rarely attended the scheduled classes, though we also tried not to overtly break the rules.

Days passed. Dawn continued to pursue being more radical. This included an evening spent with the twins, where they pleasured her together. She told me about it the next day, as we soaked in a bath, reclining close in one of the smaller pools. "Feather, you need to try it. It was... glorious, amazing, I don't have the words to describe it. Being pressed between them, with them both inside me, I've never felt so desired and needed and hot and... oh!" She shivered beside me despite the hot waters. "They were everywhere around me, hard bodies pressed against me, hands helping and caressing, lips pressing. It was pure bliss, and then... feeling them both inside me, finishing together, was the epitome of a perfect moment. I don't know how many orgasms I had, because the last one blasted them all away in a shivering, shuddering eternity of paradise." She giggled, giddy. "I've asked them back tonight. I want more!" She turned a bit serious after that though. "Mostly, I want more because... I felt so close to Bonding last night. Sex with both of them was so different and new and wonderful, and I felt everything so acutely. I know I was close to Bonding, but... it didn't happen."

"Oh, truly?"

She nodded. "I don't know if sex with two guys is enough though. Even three or more, might not do it. I grew up in a house where minor orgies were the norm."

I nodded. "I hope you find what you need."

I had had a few encounters with the brothers individually but was already starting to feel like they were getting too close. So, I'd told them both I needed a break. Then... I'd done my own scary-radical thing and asked that massive young man if he wanted to join me. His name — very appropriately — was Boulder. I'd never seen a man as large as he, and he was only nineteen years old. And he may have had a man's body, but his features were youthful, with the clearest green eyes. I'd be meeting him tonight and was jittery with anticipation.

Dawn must have felt my trembling in the bath. "What?" she asked.

"Boulder's coming to my room tonight."

She gave me a wicked grin and said, "Don't you mean Boulder's *coming in your womb* tonight?" She laughed at my wide-eyed, surprised stare at her unrestrained bawdiness. "Now that you've pointed him out to me, I don't know how I ever missed him before. He's huge, so he probably has a tummy tickler."

"A what?" I asked shocked.

"A cock so big it feels like it's in your stomach: a tummy tickler."

I gaped at her.

She laughed. "Boulder's about the size of Lord Ant, one of my mother's lovers, and she always said she needed to be extra ready for him and was always a little sore afterwards." After a moment she went on. "Tail and Agate always have some oil on them. I'll run some over to you; you may need it. If not to help him in, then to massage your aching parts after."

I playfully slapped her shoulder. "You're awful!" Though, after a moment I did concede, "Though that oil might not be a bad idea." And my parts were already beginning to ache — in a good way — in anticipation of Boulder's visit tonight.

Later that day we got the disturbing news that the

Empire of Thraan had conquered the neighboring nation of Basia to the west of Elista. They'd invaded with one of their dragon lords at the head of their army and destroyed western Basia. After that the king of Basia had surrendered and offered his daughter to the dragon lord in marriage. Everyone was a little on edge hearing this. It meant the dangerous and expansionist Empire of Thraan was now at Elista's doorstep.

I tried to put that distracting news from my head as I waited for Boulder's visit after dinner. The seamstresses had come and gone to Silverveil and while they'd been here, Dawn — ever the 'radical' — had paid hers for some extra items. One of those had been a gift to me, a shear, silken night-dress, which clung to me like a lover's embrace and showed off my form well. I was dressed only in that when Boulder's soft knock came on my shuttered window.

I opened the window to let him in. That was a challenge in itself as he squeezed and shifted to get his large form through the small opening. This resulted in him crashing to the floor in a heap, legs still sticking out the window. Not the most dashing of entrances.

I helped him up and closed the window. When I turned back, those green eyes were large as they roamed over me in the dim light of one candle and our two glowing Lumani.

He seemed just a bit stunned. "You're... beautiful," he breathed in awe. I had assumed he'd noted that previously, but perhaps my current attire was enhancing my appeal. He shifted a little, as a rather painful-looking bulge grew in his pants.

I went to him, hands on his wide chest, feeling the heavy, rounded slabs of muscle under the cloth of his shirt. Pressing myself to him gently, I whispered: "And you're very handsome."

He swallowed hard, eyes still a bit large, looking almost fearful.

I sighed softly and retreated a step. I had a suspicion but wanted to be tender in how I asked this. "Am I... your first?" I had trouble believing a strapping young man like him hadn't attracted some female attention. Just looking at his well-muscled frame was getting me all manner of hot and wet.

"Ah... oh... ah...no," he said softly. After a heavy sigh he repeated: "No." If I wasn't his first, I got the distinct impression he hadn't had good experiences so far.

I sat on the bed and motioned for him to sit next to me. He nodded and sat, the bed creaking under his weight.

"Do you want to talk about it?" I asked.

It seemed he did, as words began tumbling out of him in a rush: "My family had arranged a marriage for me. We have a large sheep farm and thought to bring our family together with a wool merchant. And even though some of the village girls had offered to lay with me, I had kept myself for my betrothed. But..." His shoulders slumped with another heavy sigh. "Well, our families thought we should meet and... ah... see what we thought of each other before the marriage. Her father gifted us with three days at a small cottage, where we'd be alone, living as if we were married to see if we would be happy together. My father didn't want to force this marriage on me but hoped I might find love with this girl and create a bond between our families." He was fully rambling now, but I didn't stop him. I sensed that he needed to get this all out. "My betrothed — her name was Ginea — she was, well, a small and delicate woman and though she appreciated my size for the labor and tasks around the house, when we lay together, she was... a bit... ah... she said I was too heavy and awkward and painful.

She... she called off the marriage. She couldn't imagine trying to have my children. I was just too big for her."

Ah.

I laid my hand gently upon his thick and rigidly muscled thigh. "I'm sorry to hear that," I said with sympathy. "It must have been hard to be turned away for something you have no control over."

He nodded. "Yeah, it was."

"And... that was the only time you were with a woman?"

He nodded.

"And... you think... you'll hurt me?" I hazarded a guess.

He hadn't been looking at me, staring at the opposite wall, but now he did. "I... don't know. I might. You're... not as small as Ginea."

Indeed.

"But you accepted my offer to be with me tonight, and you've come this far. You must at least be curious?"

He nodded quickly, swallowing hard. "I... you are... I had hoped that maybe... but..."

Spirits this man was a mess. As much as he was a manly and handsome hulk physically, emotionally he was still a scared child in many ways it seemed.

"Boulder," I said, catching his attention and he quieted. "I want to be with you. And I know you want to be with me. But this doesn't have to be anything awkward or painful. There are many ways a man can pleasure a woman, and for a woman to pleasure a man, and I'm sure we can find something which will please us both. Would you like that?"

He nodded furiously again.

I gave a soft, sympathetic laugh. "Then get up and get out of your clothes, I think you're far too uncomfortable in them, yes?"

Another nod and a hard swallow. He rose and stripped.

There was no finesse or grace to it, no play or tease, just disrobing as fast as he could.

And once he had, I could see how a small delicate woman might have had some issues. His cock was massive, certainly a 'tummy tickler' as Dawn had called it. Not only was it exceptionally long, but quite thick as well. More than that, Boulder was just large all around, heavy rounded muscle piled onto a tall, broad frame. If he'd been on top of Ginea, she'd have been half-crushed under his weight.

I rose and, seeing it only fair to match his state of dress, I slowly, lifted off the shift. After it cleared my head and I put it aside, I was just a bit stunned to see that his cock had actually gotten larger!

"Oh," I said, with a heated, dry-mouthed breath, "You are..." I didn't want to say *big*, as that might put him off. "Exceptional, aren't you?"

"So are you," he said, then he shifted a little, "So... what now?" His cock was throbbing, red and ready, but I saw the fear in his eyes.

I stepped in, reaching out to gently take his erection as I drew closer. I was not a small woman, though not particularly tall either. Still, once I was next to him the tip of his cock was resting in my cleavage. I ran my fingers up and down the top of his cock, shifting my shoulders in to press my breasts around it.

He gasped and I felt the heavy twitch of this massive erection against me.

"Do you like this?" I asked softly.

"Yes, very much," he said. Those large, heavy hands of his reached out, so very tentatively to take my shoulders, softly caressing my arms. I felt his body trembling, whether from nervousness or excitement, I couldn't tell. His rough, strong hands sent shivers through me as he caressed me. He was being so very gentle, but I felt the latent power suppressed within him.

On his own, he began a soft thrusting motion, moving his cock up and down in my cleavage. I pressed my ample softness around him more, but that's not where I wanted my hands to be. I wanted to touch him, feel his huge form. So, I found his hands and brought them to the sides of my breasts, letting him control how much my cleavage surrounded his shaft. He pressed my breasts in close, thumbs moving over my nipples, arousing them as his thrusting grew faster.

Once he was occupied with that, I leaned forward to kiss his chest. My lips were roughly at a level with his nipples. I let my hands roam his massive chest and thick, rounded shoulders and arms.

Spirits, but he was *BIG*! The heated desire I felt just seeing his form built and boiled as my fingers traced his heavy rolling muscles. My mouth went dry, even as my folds were drooling.

"You are... this is..." he seemed lost for words.

I knew he was well on his way to his first peak. I had hoped to show him some ways of pleasuring a woman which didn't require his cock, but I knew he was focused on his release now and probably wouldn't want much else. So, I lowered myself, kneeling, taking that Oh-My-Blessed-Spirits sized cock in both hands, bringing it to my lips. Luckily, he was thicker at his base then at the tip and I was able to take some of him into my mouth. Even that much was slightly awkward. I slathered my saliva over his tip with my tongue, sucking gently, taking him in as much as I could, limited by the size of my mouth. Looking up, I saw the large saucers of his eyes. He'd not been expecting this. And his pained expression let me know he was ready. My hands on his cock could feel the throbbing, next-to-bursting pressure within him.

"There are many ways a woman can please a man," I repeated. I ran the tip of my tongue over the end of his cock. "I await your pleasure," I said as invitation. I put my lips over him again, pumping both hands along that incredible shaft, while flicking my tongue over him vigorously. He didn't need any more urging than that.

His cock bucked hard, almost out of my grip and out of my mouth as his release surged over my tongue. He tasted sweet and buttery as he filled my mouth quicker than I could swallow. His hot come dripped out, over my chin, onto my chest. He was... an extremely potent young man it seemed, and I was a bit of a mess by the time he'd finished.

When I released him, he stumbled back, leaning heavily on the wall. "I've never... that was... you are... Ohhh," he breathed and blinked and stared at me.

"Ginea never thought of that, did she?" I asked, playfully as I rose. I went to a small basin of clean water and wet a cloth to clean myself. I'd brought it up from the baths earlier, just in case I'd wanted to wash off any sweat or such before I slept.

He shook his head.

Of course, if Ginea had been thinking of him as a source for children, then she wouldn't have thought to use her mouth.

"Could I... help...?" he asked, awkwardly, reaching out an arm but not moving as I wiped myself off. He knew the mess was his fault. But I was nearly done as it was, and shook my head, finishing my impromptu bath and putting the cloth away.

"Now," I asked, "would you like to learn how to pleasure me without using your cock?" Then I couldn't help but whisper, "And later, maybe we'll see how it fits, would you like that?"

He couldn't stop nodding, a look of excited curiosity on his face.

I went to him, taking his hand and drawing him to the bed. I lay back, lounging, as he sat on the edge of the bed. "Let's start with kissing and all the wonderful things you can do with your mouth."

As it turned out, Boulder was an apt pupil, quick to understand and pick things up. He was also very eager to please. Once he'd mastered kissing — a process I very much enjoyed, especially the long, lingering draws on my aroused nipples — we moved on to all the wonderful things he could do with his hands and fingers. Fingers, which were deliciously large and thick.

By then I was having troubles instructing him as I was panting and moaning between every other word. It was clear he wanted to know how to please a woman and doing a *very* good job at learning it. Every touch of those rough fingers sent thrills of carnal need through me. His heavy lips and large tongue could work wet wonders, and by that point I was sensitive all over and his kisses only stoked my fires. By the time his fingers began kneading my folds I was a slick mess, ready for a release.

With one long, thick finger inside me, his thumb slowly circled and pressed upon my clit. I shuddered and grunted — in a very non-lady-like way — as I came so hard, I pushed his finger right out of me. He returned quickly though, ensuring I was thrilled all the way through that body-churning orgasm until I was a sweaty, quivering, pool of goo in his hands.

I hoped he was ready for more. I certainly was.

"Over... there," I panted, covered in a sheen of sweat,

voice and body weak. I threw my arm out toward the bedstand. "Vial... of oil."

He understood and retrieved it. Dawn had indeed brought me some of the oil the twins always had on them, just in case. I hoped it would be enough. I dragged myself up into a sitting position at the edge of the bed and he knelt next to the bed, handing me the vial.

"So," I said, speaking slowly, giving myself a bit of time to regain myself after that earth-shattering orgasm. "If you are going to try to enter a woman with your cock, then... do what you just did, that'll make sure she's wet and worked up. But!" I said as I poured half the contents of the oil onto my cupped hand. "It may also take a bit more to make things work. I'd suggest you always have some oil on hand, like this, to make sure you're... slippery as well." And I dribbled oil from my hand onto that thick and ready shaft, then used both hands to massage it all over his significant erection.

He was a lot less awed and amazed at my touch of his cock now, sturdier and in control. I'd helped him understand all the tools he had to please a woman, and he'd learned quickly how to use them well. He had a right to be confident.

Once he was wet and gleaming in the dim light, I handed the vial to him. "And it never hurts to apply some to the lady as well. Use what you learned about your fingers to massage me with the rest of this."

He nodded, pouring the rest of the vial out onto his massive hand. I opened my legs and he pressed his three thick fingers hard against me. I shuddered with the power behind that touch, then shivered again as he began to move and caress the oil into my folds... and deeper still.

I laid back. "And when you and she are ready, take it

slow, careful, don't be afraid to ask how it feels and hope-fully she won't be afraid to tell you."

I was trembling with anticipation but had to wait precious moments longer as he finished administering the oil. I felt one of his large hands move over my legs and hips, down under my buttocks and lift me. I closed my eyes, concentrating only on his touch and...

I felt the solid bulk of his shaft settle onto my folds. I gasped, shivering with delight at the weighty press upon me. He began a slow rubbing of that massive cock over me, from thick base to swollen tip. With my eyes closed, proportions were distorted. He felt impossibly long as he slowly stroked himself from base to tip across my folds. I moaned and shuddered, partly at the pressure of his heaviness, and partly in anticipation of that *impossible* cock inside me.

"Yes," I whispered, urging him on.

He drew back, and I felt his tip poised, pressed against my quivering opening. Then there was greater pressure, a push, and...

I gasped, arching my back with the intensity of sensation as he utterly stretched me. My eyes snapped open, and he stopped, looking at me with concern. He only had his tip inside me and already it felt like I was at my limits.

"Too much?" he asked.

I shook my head quickly, not sure if I could form words.

He raised a brow, perhaps a bit surprised.

"Just... really big... and full... feels good," I gasped when I had breath again.

He laughed. "I'm barely inside you."

I rocked my hips swiveling around that massive hunk of him. "You can... really... play with... this." I lost words then, my movement over him bringing me to the brink of bliss. I was about to reach down and rub my clit to push me over the edge, but he was there first. He laid a meaty hand low on my abdomen as his thick thumb slid down to stroke my nub. I came so hard, writhing violently, that I bucked his cock out of me. His fingers replaced it quickly, vigorously stroking and drawing out the amazing orgasm, an agony of ecstasy as I squirmed and whimpered.

I was breathing hard, barely able to swallow, mouth dry, by the time I'd finished.

"Do you want more?" he asked, and I only then looked at him, the barely restrained ache on his features, the hard consistent twitching throb of that tummy-tickler of his.

"Yes," I gasped, voice hoarse. "All of you, as much as I can take." He seemed to question my decision with a look, and I turned feral on him. "Now! Before I change my mind!"

His eyes went wide and he too, took on his own feral look. He grabbed his cock and shoved it down and into me, then thrust hard, painfully, going exquisitely, impossibly deep inside me. I'd never felt anything like this, the fine line of pain and pleasure, the intensity and pressure, so full and tight and... words and thoughts blurred away. There was only one word: "Yes."

I arched my back, throwing my head back against the bed, hands out to the side, fisting the sheets. My eyes were pressed shut as I cried out my one word over and over.

I felt Boulder's heavy form over me as he leaned forward, thrusting with bestial vigor. His lips found my oh-so-aroused nipples, plucking and sucking as he drove himself, again and again, so very deep inside me. I felt a tingling in my toes and fingers then... From my core came an explosion of stunning euphoria, spreading hot tendrils of bone-jarring bliss into every part of me. My body erupted with the hardest, most muscle-gripping, skin-tingling orgasm I'd ever felt. I wrapped my legs around Boulder, pushing him as deep as he could go as I felt his last, desperate thrust, then...

He roared as he burst forth within me. Feeling his release, so hot and deep, brought a second wave of rapture radiating through me so intense I think I blacked out.

When I came to, I was panting and whimpering as he drew great gasping breaths above me. His cock was still twitching in aftershocks of pleasure and each one caused mini-orgasms to pulse through me.

His large hands rested to either side of my head, pressing into the bed, keeping him aloft over me, but he lowered himself to kiss me all over. And when his lips met mine, we pressed and played, nibbled and licked as our bodies, slowly recovered from that mind-boggling moment.

It was a long time later when he finally pulled himself out, and I felt utterly void and empty.

"I didn't hurt you?" he asked flopping down on my bed next to me. Again, the bed creaked dangerously.

"No, yes... sort of. A good pain." How to describe it? "It's like..." I decided to show him. I slapped his stomach as hard as I could and he flinched in surprise. Then I began to trace my finger gently around the impacted area. "Feel how sensitive it becomes after the pain? Like that. Only a thousand times more sensitive. You were amazing!"

He laughed, a breathy, soft thing. "*You* were amazing." He sighed. "You *are* amazing." From the corner of my eye, I saw him shaking his head. "I... after Ginea, I never imagined being with a woman could be so powerful and pleasureful. Thank you," he said. Then, softer, "Thank you."

I wasn't going to say "anytime." I didn't think I could take sex like this very often. But I did say: "You are most welcome." Then as a joke, I added. "After you've invested heavily in oils, come back and see me and I'll give you the advanced lesson."

"There's more?"

I chuckled. "There's always more."

"Oh Spirits," he breathed.

Exactly.

CHAPTER 19

FEATHER

BOULDER STAYED WITH ME THAT NIGHT, LAYING BEHIND ME, holding me close as we lay on our sides and slept. I woke feeling refreshed and full of life, if sore in spots. I rolled over in Boulder's arms. I wanted to be there, the first thing he saw when he woke. When those green eyes fluttered open, he smiled wide, though it quickly became a silly grin. "I dreamed about you, about us, last night."

"And did the dream version of me tell you that you were so achingly good that she still shivers when she thinks about you?" I pushed in to kiss him before he could answer, then whispered, "Because that's how I feel."

And between our entwined legs I felt his arousal stir.

"I ache for you," he whispered. "I dreamed that I got so hard that it was painful as I thought of you, but then, you were there and I was inside you and you took all of me. We fit so well and all my pain drained away." He quirked his face. "The next bit was strange, as dreams can be."

"Tell me," I whispered, curious.

"Ah... well, you got so excited you exploded, but then your spirit came and said that was how you were meant to die. Then your spirit and I had breakfast and we went to sheer sheep."

I laughed. "Sounds like a dream, yes." I lowered my voice to a husky purr to say. "But you nearly made me explode with pleasure last night." I felt his cock swell and twitch again and knew where this was going. I kissed him again, drawing him over me and when we parted next, I whispered, "Fingers first, then slow and gentle. We're out of oil."

He nodded. Then he took his time working me up, kissing and caressing me all over — making me feel adored and wonderful — before finally using his fingers to get me wet and ready. He made sure I'd had one release before he entered me, careful and slow. His thrusts were gentle and shallow, but with his fingers still working on the aroused nub of my clit, I found a second, warm, body-shivering orgasm. He too didn't need much to finish, we were both remembering last night and that memory was enough for us to find a quick and pleasant release.

After that we rolled over, so I could rest on him as he held me in those strong arms. We missed breakfast, but I didn't care. I felt so... safe in his arms, so at home.

Despite not wanting to have a close relationship with him, I found myself asking about his home and family.

I felt a shift in him then, something in the way he held me. There were dark memories there.

He softly kissed the top of my head, where it rested on the heaving muscles of his chest. "I didn't want to go to the Choosing, not initially," he began, voice low and soft. "My father is still strong and healthy, but our farm is large and with only him and my two younger brothers, it's a lot to work." I wanted to ask about his mother, but I said nothing.

He addressed that next. "My mother and my younger sister died with the Dream Fever this past winter."

My heart constricted. The Dream Fever had taken so many, including... "I know what that feels like," I whispered.

"You lost someone too?"

"Yes." My voice was just a breath, body trembling. He held me closer, tighter.

He went on a moment later. "After Ginea's refusal and the loss of my mother and sister, I too was lost. My father suggested I go to the Choosing. I don't know if he somehow knew I'd be Chosen, but... I was, and my life changed. Then... I met you and it changed again." He kissed my hair again. "I know we've only talked a few times before last night, but... I feel so close to you, Feather." He gave a breathy laugh and I loved the way it felt, feeling his chest and belly move beneath me. It made me smile too. "Feather and Boulder, how's that for opposites."

But we weren't opposite at all. After hearing his tale, I felt closer to him than I had before. Even if I wasn't looking for a relationship or love, I had found someone who understood the loss in my soul. Even more than our physical connection last night and this morning, I felt close to him now, like he was a part of me and I a part of him. Our shared grief united us, connecting us on a deeper level.

Oh! Feather! You did it! I heard Leoa's voice inside me, but it was different now; louder, clearer. She was... a part of me.

I had Bonded with her.

Leoa's energy and spirit infused me. I felt stronger, more alive and in touch with my senses, which were all tingling now. Given my position, with my naked body pressed to Boulder, his arms around me, everywhere we touched I felt thrills surge through me.

I breathed out a long and shuddering: "Ohhh."

"Feather?" Boulder asked.

"I just Bonded," I whispered.

"Oh?"

I smiled, knowing he couldn't see it, and I laughed a little. I felt, with all he'd gone through he needed another boost so I whispered. "Yeah, I guess sex with you was so good it made me Bond with my Lumani."

He chuckled. "Something tells me there's more to it than that, but... thanks."

Oh Feather, this is wonderful! And I can already tell you are going to be a powerful host. I can feel it in every fiber of our being. I can already sense the presence of a spirit-gift.

A spirit-gift? What's that?

A rare and precious thing. When the right True-Bonding happens and the pair of human and Lumani is strong, their purpose fixed, they can share a special power. I don't know what yours will be yet, but I can feel it budding, growing.

Oh... wow. I'd never thought of myself as particularly strong, nor with a fixed purpose, but then... I did feel, so different now. I'd connected with Dawn when we'd gone to the Mists, and now I'd connected with Boulder. And somehow that had Bonded me to Leoa and I felt like... that was just the start. That I would connect with so many more people. When I'd been in the Mists, I'd felt a connection with all things: my purpose. I was suddenly very curious what this spirit-gift would be and how it would manifest, but for now... I simply rested in Boulder's arms and marveled at these new connections.

I knew I'd not be able to let go of Boulder as easily as I had the twins. Not now. But how did I explain that to him? "Boulder," I began slowly. "I think... I'd like it if we got to know each other a bit more. I... I'd told you before I'm not looking for love, but I'm hoping we can be... close friends?" I didn't like the question in my voice. "I want to be friends... who also have sex. I know that sounds odd, but—"

He put a large finger to my lips silencing my awkward ramblings. "I'd like that," he whispered. "We'll figure it out. Thank you."

I hoped he understood. As he'd said, we'd figure it out.

"Thank you," I whispered back to him and relaxed fully upon him. We remained close, in bed, for the entire morning, finally rising and dressing to make it to the great hall for the midday meal.

Dawn joined us as we began to eat, a knowing grin on her face. "Did you two sleep well last night?" she asked with mock innocence. "Exhausted, were you?"

I skipped over her questions and told her the important thing: "I Bonded this morning."

Her eyes wend wide. Her Lumani, still in the form of the odd-looking rodent, on her shoulder twitched its whiskers. "Truly," she breathed. "Oh, Feather, I'm so happy for you!" She laid a hand on mine with a wide smile. "You need to tell someone. You need to get your true name!"

Oh yes. I'd forgotten about that. I had only just gotten used to being Feather. "I'll get to that," I said with a hint of a laugh. I turned to Boulder. "Boulder and I also... sort of bonded this morning. I think... I think it was connecting with him that helped me Bond with Leoa." I put my free hand on his, so much larger. A faint shiver ran through me at the remembrance of what he could do with those thick fingers.

When I looked back at Dawn, she had one brow raised, a half-smile on her face. I silently thanked her for not making a crude joke about 'bonding' with Boulder. It hadn't been that sort of a moment, but something far deeper. Instead, I asked, "How was your evening with the twins?"

Her half-smile pulled into a full grin. "Amazing," she said, but then her smile faded, brow furrowing as she looked down. "Truly amazing, but... I'm no closer to Bonding."

Ah. I could almost feel her sorrow and the frustration laden beneath her words.

"I'm sorry."

She took a long breath and forced a smile. "But I'm so happy for you! We should go to the headmaster right away for your name!"

I nodded. "Let's go," I said. I'd only nibbled at my lunch, despite a raging hunger. I was just too full of my own stirred up emotions to feel the needs of my body.

Boulder rose when I did. "Are you coming with us?" I asked. I wouldn't mind that.

He gave a wide smile. "No, I have my own work to do. I still need to Bond. I'll catch up with you later today." He stepped in and wrapped those strong arms around me, surrounding me with his strength in a gentle embrace and I sunk into him, feeling more at home in his arms than I had anywhere... since Davas had died.

Oddly. That thought didn't stir up the usual intensity of pain and grief. I was a bit surprised at this, but then I understood. I loved Davas and mourned him, but what I'd been truly mourning had been my loss of connection, which had been restored. I sighed. My soul still had a lot of mending to do around Davas, but that process had begun in truth this morning. "I'll see you later," I said. He released me and bent down for a quick, soft kiss.

I left him there as Dawn and I hurried across campus to the headmaster's office in the administration building.

"Do you love him?" Dawn asked.

"I do," I said, surprising myself with that answer. I hadn't been looking for love. Yet, I also knew that this was not true romantic love, not yet. "I love him... like I love you. He is close to me now. We still need to figure out exactly what we're both feeling and how whatever we have is going to work."

"So, does that mean you're done with the twins?" Dawn asked.

"Why? You want them both for yourself?"

"Maybe... but also, they've inquired about you, Agate in particular. I think you truly affected him."

I hadn't realized I'd had that much of an effect on him... on them.

"And you wouldn't mind losing him?"

She laughed. "Oh, I wouldn't lose him. He, well, both of them seem intent on sharing us."

"Oh! Is that an option?" It's what we'd done so far, but still...

"My mother would say so."

Right, the queen had her own little harem of lovers.

We arrived at the headmaster's office and were quickly admitted. The headmaster — Master Rook — was a bookish woman, small of frame with spectacles and salt-and-pepper hair pulled back in a tight bun. I'd heard she was the Master of the Library at Miraline. Yet, for the few months of the year when Silverveil was in session, she organized and oversaw the proceedings here. Despite her severe look she had a warmth which matched her intellectual intensity and smiled at us as we sat before her desk.

"Feather Bonded!" Dawn blurted, and I laughed.

Rook nodded to me. "Congratulations. Have you chosen a name, or has one been chosen for you?"

I looked at Dawn, who shrugged.

The name one received was based off of the avatar

animal they'd chosen. Sometimes it was overt, like Master Rook, and sometimes it was based off an ability or attribute of that animal, like Queen Legs. The trouble was... neither Dawn nor I knew what animal we'd chosen.

I sheepishly admitted as much to Master Rook.

"And your Lumani doesn't know?"

Nope. It is a rodent of some form, but of the exact species I am uncertain.

"No."

Rook's dark brows rose. "That is odd indeed." She huffed a sigh. "I don't suppose you are able to take your avatar form yet? I am familiar with nearly all of the worlds fauna and might be able to identify it."

How do I transform? I asked Leoa

Think upon the form I had, imagine yourself in that form. Think of it like when you were in the Mists, if you believe it strong enough it will happen.

I closed my eyes, concentrating. Alas, my Bonding must have still been too new and I was unable to take the shape.

"It looks like this," Dawn said.

I opened my eyes to see her holding her Lumani.

Right! I'd forgotten we shared an avatar form.

"Looking similar to another creature doesn't mean much in the rodent world," Rook said.

"No, we have the same avatar," I said quickly.

Headmaster Rook blinked, looking from Dawn to me. "That is unheard of. It is rare enough to have two True-Bonded with the same avatar even across generations. There have never been two who were Chosen at the same time, who took the same avatar."

"It's true," Dawn insisted. She pushed on. "You know how we snuck out to go to the Mists early." A shadow crossed Rook's face, but she nodded. "Well, afterward Amya had taken this avatar form, and Feather and I knew that we were the same. We think it has something to do with how we're both seeking connection as part of our purpose in Bonding. I can't explain it, but you have to trust me."

I sensed something then, an odd joyous delight from Leoa, which I didn't understand.

Rook nodded. She looked at me. "I wish to speak to your Lumani."

I blinked.

Don't worry, I know what to do, I'm going to take control of your body for a moment. You will be well, trust me. Her voice was light and excited. I sensed there was more behind her wish to take control than just the headmaster's request.

I do trust you, go ahead.

And Leoa swelled, filling me, taking control of my physical form. "Yes, I am Leoa. Speak," she said, and I was just a little surprised at how commanding my voice could be.

I saw something in Dawn's features twitch, surprised, but couldn't do anything about it with Leoa in control.

"Do you confirm this? Your form is the same as Dawn's Lumani?" Rook asked.

"Yes, Headmaster. A rodent of some form, but one with which I am not familiar."

Rook nodded. "Thank you, that is all."

But Leoa didn't leave right away, instead we turned to Dawn. "Dawn, you said your Lumani's name was Amya?"

Dawn was smiling in a strange way. "Yes... and... he knows you."

Leoa nodded. "Indeed. We have been... very close... through our True-Bonded, in the past." Leoa was practically bubbling over with joy.

"Amya says he is overjoyed to be with you again, and... and he's so very happy Feather and I have become friends."

"I am overjoyed as well, that Amya and I have found each other once again." I could feel the wide smile of trembling elation and love upon my face. "We'll talk more later. Thank you, Dawn," Leoa said and retracted back inside me, giving me control of my body once again.

What was that about? I asked Leoa.

Sometimes it is hard for Lumani to recognize each other in our energy forms, especially outside of the Mists. But Amya and I have been close, several times, in our previous lives, our hosts were married once and lovers in other lives. We... love each other.

Oh! I smiled. *Then I'm so very happy Dawn and I are close and you get to be near each other again! I don't think we'll become lovers though.*

No, I know. Still, it is nice to know we are together again.

With that revelation out of the way, Rook asked Dawn: "Please place your Lumani upon my desk I wish to study them."

Dawn did as instructed.

Rook looked closely at the cute little creature. It was a bit hard to see its true shape because it was a being of fiery red and orange energy. Still, she seemed to see something which made sense to her and she sat back with a sigh. Her eyes looked up and away and seemed to be shifting rapidly as if reading. Someone had told me Headmaster Rook had a perfect memory, remembering everything she'd seen and read. Whether this was a natural gift or a spirit-gift was unknown, but she seemed to be using it now.

After a long moment she drew in a breath and smiled. "Ah... yes. A rare and precious animal indeed." She sat forward and took a moment to look at Dawn and me. "Feather, you and Dawn — assuming she Bonds soon as well — have chosen the form of a Kangaroo Rat."

I didn't even know what that first word was, and being a

rat didn't sound appealing. But Dawn grinned widely. She turned to me quickly. "Roo! Your name is Roo!"

I grinned. That was a pleasant name indeed.

"Roo," I repeated to myself and nodded.

The headmaster sighed looking at Dawn. "Your own selection for names may be limited being of the same species."

Dawn laughed. "Oh, I'm not changing my name. I'll just keep being Dawn."

The headmaster raised a single brow, but apparently decided not to argue the point. Instead, she said. "I can just tell you are going to turn this nation on its head, young one."

Dawn smiled. "That I will."

As we rose to leave, a messenger came rushing into the headmaster's office. Whether they didn't see us or their news was too important, I didn't know, but they blurted it out as soon as they saw the headmaster.

"Master! The groups who went to the Mists today, they've been attacked! Some have been killed and others are injured!"

Dawn and I looked at each other. I could see she was feeling the same cold dread I was. Our group had gone to the Mists today, but the two of us had been given a pass since we'd already been. But that meant... Tail was out there and might be one of those who'd been hurt or... killed!

CHAPTER 20

Dawn

Stone group, along with several guards and instructors, were sent to the Mists to help those there, while investigating the attack.

Feather — no, Roo now — and I wanted to go, but were told to stay. For once in my life, I listened. I had a horrible feeling this attack just may have been my fault. If some enemy of the state — though none of us knew who that might be — knew I was the heir, they might have been targeting me. If I went to help, I'd be playing into their hands, and that would only make everything worse. So, we waited, but waiting was horrible and frustrating. So, to distract ourselves, I taught Roo some more of the fighting style I knew. She'd been practicing her walking and already seemed more confident and graceful, just by doing that much. But, since we were both distracted, it was hard for her to learn and me to teach.

It was dusk by the time everyone returned and we knew

a bit more. The news was dire indeed: of the twelve people that had gone to the Mists — two groups — eight of them had perished. Nearly all the members of the Tree group had died including Master Roan, two of their members had survived by hiding away from the fighting. Roo and I thanked the Spirits to see Tail alive. Yet, he and Beak were the only survivors from our group. They were both children of Nobles who'd been wise enough to train their offspring in combat. The two had fought desperately, defending themselves as best they could. Master Crab had died, fighting fiercely despite his old age, protecting his students. And yet, both Plume and Wing had died as well. No one knew exactly how, since the fighting had been in the thick of the forest and it had been hard to keep track of everyone.

Yet, from those gruesome and horrible events, some small blessings had come, as many had Bonded that day.

Tail was now Swift, a bird known for its relentless flight. He had fought to the brink of exhaustion, then kept fighting beyond his limits and had Bonded with his Lumani through that extremity of endurance.

Agate was now Falcon. Even though he'd not been attacked, he'd been in the group sent to help. Knowing his brother was in trouble, he'd run as fast as he could to get there. Yet, it hadn't been fast enough, so he'd Bonded out of necessity, fearing for his twin. He'd instantly taken his avatar form as one of the fastest birds and flown quickly to aid his brother.

Boulder, also in the group who'd been sent to help, was now Rhino. He'd not Bonded on the way there, but once he'd reached the scene of the attack. He'd gathered up the survivors and carried them all — four of them — back to Silverveil. He'd needed reserves of strength he'd not possessed and his Bonding — with a rhinoceros beetle of all things — had given him the power he'd needed to keep going and heft them all with ease.

Others had Bonded as well, but there were few celebrations that night. There wasn't anyone with the true healing gift at Silverveil, so the injured were tended to and made to rest. Roo, Falcon, Rhino, and I, sat vigil over Swift as he slept. His wounds were grave and deep, but we all knew he had great strength and hoped he would pull through. Quartz — who I'd known as Eadric, my Fey friend — came by during the night. Being a part of stone group, he'd seen the massacre, but was one of the few who hadn't Bonded yet. He didn't say anything but stood beside me for a long moment, a reassuring hand on my shoulder. I nodded to him, saying a soft "thank you." He smiled and nodded, remaining stoic and saying nothing. After a while, he left. He was taking our 'time apart' seriously it seemed. I was glad for that.

The next morning, the nurses said Swift's wounds had closed well and did not seem septic. He would heal and survive.

Needing to stretch my legs — and needing to rest, but not feeling ready for that yet — I got up for a walk. Roo came with me. Rhino, also came, but walked behind us by several paces, giving us room. I think he just didn't want to let us out of his sight given the previous day's events. I could understand that. We stayed inside Silverveil's walls and walked the perimeter, ambling slowly.

We didn't speak for a long time. I was the one who broke the silence. "I'll be leaving Silverveil tomorrow," I said, certain. "I'll arrange for a fast carriage to the capital." I had been staring at the ground in front of me as I'd walked but looked up at Roo. "I want you to come with me." Before she could answer, I added, "And Swift and Falcon, and Rhino."

She raised a brow. "You haven't Bonded yet. Are you... giving up?"

"No, I'm doing something radical. Maybe that will help." I flashed her a determined grin.

She gave a half-hearted laugh. "It might. What are you thinking?"

"I'm going to go talk to... my parents... about starting a new Noble House."

Roo's eyes widened. "Starting a new Noble House and not being Bonded yet? That is bold indeed."

"I don't care if I'm Bonded, I... I want to start my plans now. I want to create a new House where we're together, all of us, and we're... safe." I looked away. I couldn't shake the feeling that the attack yesterday had somehow been my fault: people looking for me. And, I didn't know if it would have made things worse or better if I'd been there. A part of me thought I could have helped, saved lives. But given the description of the relentless attackers, I wasn't entirely sure of that.

Roo sighed heavily. "You blame yourself for the attack." It wasn't a question and I hadn't mentioned my concerns to her, so I was a bit surprised at this.

I looked up at her, shocked. "Yes, how...?"

She pulled me close in a side-long embrace. "I can feel it. I'm starting to truly connect with people around me and because I'm closest to you, I feel you the most. I sensed your pain and frustration and... guilt."

She was growing so far beyond the girl I'd met that first day at Silverveil, so much more confident and... powerful.

I nodded. "If anyone knows who I am, and has a grudge against my parents, or either of the countries to which I'm linked, and if they'd known our group would be at the Mists that day...?" I trailed off. It may have been arrogant and self-centered to think this was my fault, but I couldn't get that fear out of my head and heart.

We stopped walking then. Roo nodded, shifting to hold me closer, warm and reassuring. I rested my head upon her soft bosom while she stroked my hair and rubbed my back. She said nothing, just let me have my moment and eased my suffering with her presence.

"Thank you," I whispered when I finally began to feel myself again. I pulled back with a heavy breath. "But I still intend to head to the capital tomorrow. Are you with me?"

She smiled. "I am. Though Swift may not be fit to travel. He's still healing. And I don't think Agate — I mean Falcon — would leave his brother here alone." She cocked her head to one side. "But they are both birds, and fast ones, they could catch up to us quickly once Swift is healed."

I nodded. I didn't like it. I wanted all of my friends there with me when I confronted my mother, but Roo was right.

We continued to walk, our unending circle. I didn't quite know how to say this next bit, but eventually I gave up on trying to make it sound good and just said it. "Usually, a House needs to prove itself to be accepted for membership, do something significant for the nation. I was thinking we could... go to Thraan and make peace with them, make sure they don't invade us." There, it was said, my insane plan.

Roo tilted her head for a sidelong look at me. "Go to Thraan? Where they marry the princesses of the countries they take over? And you being a princess? Does that seem wise?"

I smiled. "Since when have I worried about being wise?"

Roo nodded, then sighed heavily. "I should have known this would come. Being your friend means doing some wild and crazy things." She shrugged. "Sure, why not, let's go conquer the empire with kindness and diplomacy."

"Exactly," I said with a firm nod. I didn't feel half as confident as I was letting on... and both Roo and I knew it.

This would be a dangerous and intricate endeavor, but if I could pull it off, I'd be guaranteed my new House.

Now, I just had to convince my mother to let me do it.

CHAPTER 21

DAWN

WE LEFT THE NEXT DAY, NOT LONG AFTER THE GATES OF Silverveil opened. Word had been passed around that a message about the recent attack needed to be sent to the capital and a fast carriage arranged. It was partially the truth, but the headmaster had seen wisdom in not letting many know of my movements. She might not have been convinced that the attack at the Mists was my fault, but she did consider it a possibility. So, we rode in secret, Roo and I, with Rhino as our guard.

Falcon saw us off, embracing Roo and me. Swift was doing better and their plan was to join us in the capital in about a week or so. Swift still wouldn't be fully healed by then, but with healers coming up from Miraline to aid with the wounded, he'd hopefully be well enough to fly, assuming he could take his avatar form.

It would take us about five days to get to the capital by fast carriage. I had that time to prepare exactly what I'd say to my mother.

But...

By the time we arrived, I still had no clue. Roo's advice was: "Be direct, it's what you do best." She was right, of course, but... I hadn't seen my parents in eight years. A part of me was afraid, once I was back in their presence, I'd become that uncertain and insecure child once again.

The carriage brought us directly to the Spider House Estate in the capital. Even if I wouldn't be speaking with my mother today, I'd still be staying here. I drew just a little bit of joy from the wide-eyed wonder on both Roo and Rhino's faces as we rode through the capital, and at the sight of the Estate.

"These grounds are as large as my entire village back home," Roo breathed.

The carriage let us out under a massive, covered carriage porch, and I guided my friends to the wide stairs, nodding to Halloran, the Doorman. He blinked a little at me, recognition coming after a moment. "Mistress Dawn?"

"I'm back," I said with a grin.

"I'll go tell your parents!" he said with a snap of his heels. He opened the door for us, but then was off.

"You grew up here?" Roo asked in awe.

"Here and at Hedgewild, the estate in the south."

"Wow," she breathed.

Rhino was a massive silent statue behind us, also taking this all in. I'd learned a lot about him during this trip: his family's sheep farm and his lost mother and sister, and far too much about sheep-shearing. He was a good man, and even had a subtle wit about him, which I admired. And he was easy on the eyes as well, that big frame, easy smile, and those sparkling green eyes. I was curious if Roo and he were into sharing, though given what Roo had told me about how well-endowed he was, I didn't really know if I was up for that or not.

The carriage driver brought in our few things and we waited in the massive foyer... for quite a while... before a line of people in fine clothes filed out passed us. Not long after that, my mother and father showed up. Lady Sparrow was with them, beside my mother, as was Lord Ant, flanking my father. They didn't look that much different from how I remembered them. The King was the least affected by age, given his Fey heritage. His hair was still raven black. All the others had touches of gray or silver in their dark hair. There were a few more lines, perhaps, upon my mother's face — ruling two nations did wear on a person — and the bags under her eyes were a bit darker and heavier. She still carried herself with poise, however, those russet brown eyes still keen. Of all of them, Ant seemed to have fared the worst while I was away. He'd lost some of his bulk, thinner, muscles sagging a little. Perhaps he'd been sick? Or perhaps the trials of helping my parents rule two countries simply wore on him harder. Sparrow was still small and pristine, forest green eyes intent upon me. It was in those eyes that I saw the most disappointment, which stung. I had always been close with the small woman, even when Mother hadn't been there for me, Sparrow had, most of the time. Of all of them, I feared her scorn the most, and it seemed I had earned it.

"Dawn," Mother said softly. "It's good you have returned." Her brow furrowed, though as her gaze settled upon Amya perched on my shoulder. "You... haven't Bonded yet?"

"My friends and I are weary from the road. Might we freshen up before you yell at me?" I said, probably with just a tad too much petulance in my voice. I definitely wasn't being my old self, except for the bit where my parents seemed to bring out the worse in me.

"Yes, of course. Sparrow, please see them to their rooms." And that was it. Mother and Father turned away, Ant trailing behind them as they left. They whispered to each other, and my father shook his head. I wondered what they were saying.

"Your mother can't figure out if she wants to hug you or punish you," Roo said softly.

Everyone looked at her.

She shrugged. "Kangaroo rats have exceptional hearing."

Sparrow gave her a harsh look. "It is not becoming of a young lady to eavesdrop on her queen."

Roo nodded. "Apologies."

Sparrow, without another word, led us up a grand set of stairs to the second floor. Roo and Rhino were given a small suite with two rooms, and I was returned to the room I'd had as a child. That room had far too many bad memories for me, however, so once Sparrow was gone, I snuck over to Roo and Rhino's rooms. They were both half-dressed, bodies entwined and kissing passionately as I entered. I probably should have expected that. This was the first time they'd been alone in five days.

Roo, however, smiled and covered herself when she saw me, no malice in those soft sable eyes.

"I'm going to use your washing room, if that is well with you. I... can't be in my old room." I shuddered.

"By all means," Roo said and motioned to the large bathing room off the main common area of the suite. "Rhino and I may be... a little while in the shower, so you should probably go first."

I nodded with a knowing grin, then went to wash up.

It was dark once we had all had a turn, Roo and Rhino looking just a bit flushed after their mutual 'washing.'

Sparrow returned a short while later. She wore a stunning, purple evening dress and invited us to dinner. I had expected this and told the others to wear their finest, which as it turned out, wasn't that fine, but they wore it well. Roo had a simple summer dress with a bright floral print, not a ball gown at all, but it looked pretty on her. Rhino was in slightly too short and too tight pants — muscles straining the fabric — and a simple white shirt... which wasn't as white as it once had been.

And as such, we marched to war...

...or rather dinner.

Lord Silence wasn't there. As head of the nation's spy network, he was often away. That meant it was just the four of them — Mother, Father, Sparrow, and Ant — and three of us at the table. No one spoke. Dinner was eaten in a heavy silence, and it was only once the sipping wine had been poured and the main dishes taken away that Sparrow finally spoke.

"You had us all so worried! Why would you run off like that?" And there it was.

I leveled a steady gaze upon her. This was one question I had been preparing to answer for five years: "If you have to ask what drove me away, then you'll never understand my reasons." That got several stunned and confused looks. As I suspected, they did not understand.

"Drove you away?" Mother asked softly.

"Yes, Mother, drove me away. You all did. I don't have the time or inclination to describe to you what my childhood was like. You were hardly there, I was kept to safe activities, restricted in all things, even seeing my own parents. So, when I had the chance, I helped myself to a large dose of freedom." Before anyone could respond to that, I pushed on.

"And don't mistake me returning now as some attempt at reconciliation. As far as I'm concerned, that is for you to seek from me. I am here for one purpose only, to seek Queen Leg's approval in creating a new Noble House." There, I'd said it.

Stunned faces greeted me. So, I continued, emboldened by my progress so far. "I would like to create—" I hesitated for only a moment. I'd debated long and hard on the exact name of the House. Kangaroo Rat House was long and a bit confusing and I liked the short form better. "—Rat House." Yeah, that's what my house would be, the low-lifes and misfits, like Maverick House had been long ago. Spider House was no longer a home for the wayward and weird. All that had changed when my mother had become queen. There was a void, a need to take in the odd-ducks and nonconformists, and I'd fill it. "And I've already devised the perfect test for my new House, a worthy task and a challenging one, which shall prove my worth and the worth of Rat House."

"Oh?" Was all my mother said, clearly skeptical, but also curious.

"Yes. I... we, will go to the heart of Thraan and make peace with their Emperor, ensuring they will never threaten our borders."

That got the response I thought it would: gaping mouths and wide eyes. I loved it when poised, proud Royals wore those silly, astounded expressions.

"You... can't be serious," Sparrow managed to say. "That's a death sentence, or a marriage sentence, given how they've conquered some lands. We can't allow the daughter of the queen and the heir to Vauphan to be captured by the Thraians! They'd have the perfect bargaining chip to use against us. You'd be putting us in an impossible position!"

I couldn't help myself, the words just slipped out: "I would have thought the four of you were used to impossible positions."

Ant choked on his wine.

Mother actually smiled at that, it was just a hint, a twitch of her lip and then gone, but I caught it.

"Is that all you can do, make jokes?" Sparrow stormed on. "This is serious. We'd never allow—"

"Sparrow, please," Mother finally said softly with a raise of her hand. Sparrow quieted and we all waited for what the queen had to say. She looked at me for a long time. Then she looked at Roo and Rhino. "You never introduced us," she said softly.

That had not been what I was expecting and threw me for a moment. That was Mom, keeping me off balance. I sputtered a little as I said: "Ah... this is soon-to-be Lady Roo, a dear friend and solemn companion. With her, is soon-to-be Lord Rhino, another friend and our protector on the journey here." They nodded in turn.

"It is a pleasure to meet you both," Mother said with a nod of her own. "I had been told of your arrival of course, but formal introductions are always a bit more personal, don't you think?" She gave a small smile. "In case you didn't know the others here, this is Lady Sparrow." Sparrow nodded. "Lord Ant." He gave a quick bow of the head. "And finally, King Alvere and I, Queen Legs, would like to formally welcome you to the Spider House estates."

"We're honored, thank you," Roo said, sounding so noble and poised I almost didn't recognize her voice.

With that out of the way my mother looked to me, and once again there was a long pause as she studied me. "You are correct," she said softly. "Your father and I were not the parents you deserved. I am not quite sure when we forgot that duty to family should always come before duty to our nations." She sighed. "We were new... well, I was new to the role of Royal. Perhaps I was too young to be queen and mother at once. I failed you, I'm sorry."

I blinked. I hadn't expected an apology.

But... they'd also had five years to think about why I'd run off and what to say.

"Thank you," I said softly, my heart aching just a little. A part of me wanted to jump up, run over to my mother, and hug her, but I restrained myself. I felt more vindicated than soothed by my mother's words. Still, somewhere deep within me, the walls I'd put up to keep my heart safe began to crack, just a little.

Roo reached over and slipped her hand in mine under the table. She smiled softly and I felt... something odd in the moment, a brush upon my soul. It was like the emotional equivalent of someone stroking my hair or my back, soothing me. I gained strength and peace from that strange soul-touch and looking in Roo's dark eyes, I knew, somehow, it had been her. I smiled, thanking her silently for the strength.

Silence hung over the table for a long moment before my mother spoke again. "Something tells me, that we're not going to talk you out of this crazy plan to go to Thraan are we?"

I shook my head. "No." Crazy or not, I was set on my path.

"And as for the Noble House..." She grimaced. "You're not even Bonded yet. It's unheard of for someone who has not yet Bonded to form a Noble House."

I had thought about this. "True, but you have always been a progressive queen. Why is it that we restrict ourselves to True-Bonded as Nobles? Isn't that what led to the disaster that was Merlin and her followers? I know that Lumani make us stronger and wiser, but that doesn't mean that there aren't incredibly devoted and intelligent people out there who couldn't contribute immensely to the nation. So why not open up the Noble Houses to everyone?"

Mother's eyes grew wide as I saw the logic in that sink in.

"Or, if that's too radical, then Roo can be the head of my House for now. I guess it wouldn't be my House in that case, but she and I share an avatar, so the name would be the same."

I hadn't told Roo I might suggest this and I saw her pale with surprise. I winked at her.

"You have the same Avatar?" Sparrow asked softly, confusion and curiosity mixing in her voice.

"Yeah, long story. We'll save that for later," I said, not wanting to get side-tracked.

"Both of your suggestions for the establishment of the new Noble House are admirable," Mother said, nodding. "I will... consider it."

That was a good start.

Mother turned to Sparrow. "Please cancel the Council meetings for the next two days I will be spending that time with my daughter as she tells me all about her travels. I don't care what you have to do to make that work."

I blinked, stunned. Sparrow looked just as shocked.

Mother looked back to me. "And in two days' time I'll give you your answer. It is customary for new Nobles to show the House Leaders what they can do, this will give you some time to show me who you really are." She smiled sadly. "And for me to finally get to know my daughter."

Another crack formed in my emotional defenses as my

mother smiled at me in that moment. It was my smile; I could see the likeness. She'd just put her life on hold... for me. I didn't know how I felt about that. I just knew I had two days to show them who I was and convince them I should go to Thraan, so I was going to make the most of it.

CHAPTER 22

FEATHER / ROO

I wrote a letter to Swift and Falcon, telling them we'd be here for two days, then — with luck — heading for the western border. It was an eight-to-ten-day trip from the capital by fast carriage. I hoped they'd be able to join us before we left the capital, but this way, they'd know where we were if they needed more time for Swift to heal. Assuming they were flying, covering the distance from Silverveil to the western border shouldn't take them longer than roughly three days.

I also wrote a short letter to my sister, to let her know I had Bonded and was doing well. I didn't know when I would return home, but I promised I would when I could.

While Dawn spent time with her parents, Rhino and I had time to ourselves, though the first day, we were taken on an extended shopping trip. Lady Sparrow escorted us and helped us pick out a few items. We'd need to have a whole wardrobe of clothes if we were to be Nobles representing Elista. It must have cost a fortune, but we were well outfitted. I now had several nice dresses, and several more functional outfits for travelling. I also began to wear light hose under my skirts and dresses. One of the abilities I was discovering from my avatar was a significant ability to leap. I could jump over a hundred feet into the air, but doing so while wearing a skirt or dress meant when I came down, I'd show everything to the world. So, hose it was.

After the shopping trip, Rhino and I took a long, luxurious shower together. We liked the shower. I could stimulate him however he liked and any mess was quickly washed away. Afterward, he'd put his amazing fingers to good use until I was a pile of goo. Then we rested a bit before lunch.

That afternoon, we had our informal Noble's Test. A small group of House Leaders, those who were local to the capital, gathered to see what we could do. The legendary Lady Skyfire was there, still copper-haired despite her age, and she may have been gnarled and wrinkled, missing an arm and part of her chest, but she was as spry as all the tales told. Lady Dove attended as well, the queen's sister, looking radiant in white, her flowing blond hair still somehow pristine and untouched by age. Lady Blackclaw, friend of the Queen and second of House Grizzly, also made the trip to the capital to watch us. That was it for the High Nobles, though.

I showed off my leaping and enhanced — still amazing to me — reflexes as well as my incredible hearing by having them carry on a conversation in increasingly quieter tones and repeating it back to them. I could also go without water, which was hard to show, however.

Rhino lifted heavy things, then... heavier things. That was pretty much it for him.

Dawn had still not Bonded, but she gave a long talk, telling of the many places she'd been and the cultures she'd encountered and what she'd learned. Oddly, I think the assembled ladies found that far more fascinating than Rhino's or my abilities.

There was an informal dinner afterward, filled with Skyfire's rude humor, quiet tales from Dove, and Blackclaw's stories of when the queen was still at Silverveil. They were an interesting group.

That evening, Rhino and I walked to a hill outside the city and watched the sunset. He held me close, and we stole kisses like secret lovers.

We returned to the estate to find Dawn asleep on the long couch in the common area of our suite. She woke when we entered and told us about her day, spent with her parents. I could feel some of the long-time wounds in her soul starting to heal. She was happier than I'd ever seen her and, if possible, even freer of spirit.

Rhino and I retired to our separate rooms, but Dawn followed me to mine and we curled up together on the large bed, like we had that night after first experiencing the twins.

"Rhino," she said softly. "Is he interested in... sharing?" Dawn asked, voice a conspiratorial whisper. "Are you?"

I giggled a little. "I need to talk to him about it. I am, yes, but I don't know how he feels." I was a little surprised though. "I honestly don't know how well you and he would... ah... fit," I said candidly.

"Lots of oil?" she said, sounding a bit giddy and hopeful.

"Even if you both oiled yourselves to within an inch of your lives, I'm not sure how well it would go."

"It would be a lot of slippery fun to find out, though. We could just use our hands as well. Mostly I'm just... curious. He is so big and handsome and I have to admit I'm just a bit jealous of you two and your long showers."

I was fairly certain I blushed at that, even while I smiled and warmed at those memories.

I countered with, "You've had the twins at the same time, I haven't tried that yet."

"Would you like to?"

Would I? I considered for a moment. "Yes," I admitted, a bit giddy myself at the thought.

"Anyone else you've got your eye on?" Dawn asked, those luminous golden eyes filled with mischievous curiosity.

"No, but I think I caught someone's eye today?"

"Oh?" Dawn was instantly on alert. "Who?"

"He was introduced as Lord Ceph? The tall one, lanky and lean, with the long face, enigmatic eyes, and a tousle of dark hair." She nodded. "He was there at breakfast and attended to the ladies during the testing and at dinner. From what I could tell he couldn't keep his eyes off me." I lowered my tone, though I wasn't sure why exactly. "I could even *feel* his desire for me!"

"More of your spirit-gift developing?" she asked.

I nodded. More and more I was starting to sense the stronger emotions of those around me. With Dawn, having known her longer, the emotions didn't need to be as strong. It was... illuminating to say the least.

Dawn grew a bit more somber for a moment. "Thank you, for last night, after dinner, you... touched my soul, I think? It was much appreciated."

I smiled. I hadn't known if she'd felt that. I'd felt her usual strength, but also a new vulnerability, and wanted to support her. I was glad she'd felt my emotional support. "I will always be there for you," I whispered.

"And I you," she breathed.

After that we both settled into a pleasant sleep.

The next day, Rhino and I accompanied Dawn, spending the morning in a crash-course of Elistan politics. Mostly, it was what we'd need to know if Queen Legs decided to allow us to go to Thraan. I was hopelessly lost, but Rhino seemed to catch most of it and Dawn soaked it up easily. I'd need her to explain it to me in simpler terms later on. What I did glean from that morning, was that things were a lot more complex than I'd ever known, especially with Vauphan. I felt Dawn open up emotionally just a bit more as the morning progressed, perhaps finally understanding the immensity of her parents' duties to these two nations.

Dawn spent the afternoon with her parents, while Lady Dove showed Rhino and I a pleasant place to walk along the river and told us all the secret stories of the queen as a child.

And as the day drew to a close and Dawn joined me in my bed once more, I felt her mounting trepidation. Tomorrow, the queen would give us her decision on our Noble House and the trip to Thraan. Dawn was terrified her mother wouldn't let us go.

I was terrified that she would.

CHAPTER 23

DAWN

IT WAS TIME FOR MY MOTHER'S DECISION. ROO, RHINO, AND I were gathered in the formal audience chamber. Father sat next to Mother, looking tired. In the last two days I had learned so much about them, including the incredible toll it took running both countries. Vauphan's nobles were in a state of near revolt. My father had been trying for years to change the hereditary noble families to elected nobles, like here in Elista, but they had fought him tooth and nail to keep power within their families. I'd gotten the most basic summary of Vauphani politics yesterday and it boggled my mind. I'd potentially inherit that someday. A mess with no easy resolution.

Fun.

It did make me understand the pressures my parents were under a bit more, though that didn't excuse how distant they'd been during my childhood.

Sparrow and Ant were in attendance today, as were several other members of the Royal House, including Ceph, the one who couldn't keep his eyes off Roo. He seemed aloof and distant, though he wasn't without his charms. Despite being tall and gangly in appearance, he wasn't awkward in his movements as some lanky men were. I suspected he'd been tall for a while and was used to his lean frame. He was handsome, in his own way, with that unkept boyish tousle of dark hair and dark, mysterious eyes. I hoped he was getting a good look at Roo now though, since one way or another Roo and I would be leaving soon, either to Thraan or... anywhere but here. I didn't know what I'd do if Mother refused my request, but I knew I'd need a bit of time away from them again.

I stood as tall as I could, dressed in my finest white silken blouse and black leather pants, with high boots and a green vest. Roo was resplendent in red, a color which set off her darker skin. The dress accentuated her bust, drawing tight beneath her full bosom to hug her curves to where a skirt flared out below. Rhino was jaw-dropping in a shirt of dark green, which should have been billowing but instead clung to his rounded muscles, and cream-colored pants that hugged his butt and strong legs without being 'tight.'

There were a few guests in the gallery as well, this was to be a formal proclamation and everyone waited with hushed breath for the queen's words.

My mother rose, stunning in her gold armor, what she usually wore for formal events. Her voice was clear and carried as she began to speak. "Thank you all for coming today. As you may know, a formal request was made to add a new Noble House to the lists. In the interests of clarity and truth, this request was made by my daughter, Dawn, who is not a True-Bonded, and therefore, not a Noble, so I must deny her request."

I clenched my teeth, trying not to show my anger.

"However!" Mother said quickly. "A new Noble House will be born today."

Ah... so she'd gone *that* route.

"Lady Roo, step forward."

Roo — who'd been practicing the walk I'd taught her — moved gracefully to the bottom of the dais upon which my mother stood, and there she bowed down to one knee. Luckily, I'd mentioned to Roo this might happen and gone over some of the details she'd need to know.

"Since no Noble House is confirmed until they have completed a quest for the nation, I grant you the title of Acting High Noble and House Leader. Please rise and name your second."

Roo rose gracefully and addressed the queen. "Your Majesty, I name Lady Dawn to be my second."

Lady? Technically I wasn't a lady yet.

My mother nodded. "And name your House."

"House Rat, your Majesty."

"And what do you propose as your quest to prove your House's worth?"

Roo drew in a long breath. "Your Majesty, we will ensure the safety of Elista's western border, by seeking a pact of non-aggression with Thraan."

There were gasps and murmurs from the crowd.

"We accept your quest and wish you Spirits' speed upon your journey."

That was it, it was done.

My mother then quirked a bit of a smile. "I have sensed a need for a new Noble House for some time," she said, speaking to the crowd. "And I believe House Rat will be as House Maverick once was, a haven for the wayward and awkward among us... like my daughter, who isn't even Bonded yet."

Ouch. But... a valid point.

"And on that note, another proposal was made to me

recently, to allow non-True-Bonded into Noble Houses. I believe there is merit to this request and will take it into advisement with the Council of Lords and Elders." She looked at me for the briefest moment and I saw pride in her gaze. I stood a little taller. "It is my hope that someday, the best among us, not just True-Bonded will have a say in all aspects of government of this great nation!"

The crowd cheered.

The three of us were dismissed from our prominent place in the audience chamber and a few other matters were discussed before the session was ended. Once the crowd had left, the three of us were called forward again. My parents came down from the dais to speak to us privately.

"We're still very concerned for your safety," my father began.

"So, we're going to send a few representatives from our House with you, as aids in this matter," Mother said, and before I could speak, added. "This is non-negotiable, accept it."

I nodded. I didn't know what I thought of this yet.

"We'll be sending an honor guard with you, twelve men, along with Lady Midnight and—" Mother cocked her head to the side. "There has been another who volunteered to go with you: Lord Ceph."

I tried not to smile at that.

Mother sighed heavily. "Understand, we're only allowing this because we know you're going to do it anyway and this way we get to send help." She gave a half-hearted smile. "You *are* my daughter and, in my day, this would have been the sort of crazy thing I'd have done. I know I can't stop you, there is too much of me in you."

I shrugged. "So... this is your fault?"

She glared at me, then sighed. "Probably." She drew me

close into a tight embrace. "Please be careful. You're our only child, and we can't lose you."

"I'll protect her — protect them both — with my life," Rhino said nearby.

Mother nodded with a smile. "I'm sure you will, Lord Rhino, thank you." There was something in how she gave the big man a once over with her eyes that made me want to slap her. She was twice his age! But... I couldn't blame her, so I let it slide.

That night we ate dinner together as a family once more, and probably for the last time for quite a while, since it was a many-week journey to the heart of Thraan. Mother told tales of her youth. Father corrected her on the details. Sparrow blushed at some more intimate bits, and Ant sat back in his chair with a faint smile of nostalgia. This... *this* was the home I'd never had. There had never been many of these sorts of dinners, not with everyone at the table. The few times it had happened, the discussion was more often about the politics of the day than about family. I held that evening in my heart and cherished it.

Slowly, ever so slowly, the walls I'd put up around my heart were breaking down. But it was going to take more than a few pleasant dinners to ease the pain in my soul at the loss of my childhood.

A pigeon arrived while we were at dinner. Swift was mended. He and Falcon would arrive the next day. Roo and I decided we'd wait the extra day for them. I warmed with anticipation of their arrival and grew ever more nervous and excited for the quest to come.

CHAPTER 24

RHINO

I DIDN'T KNOW WHAT I'D DONE — WHAT GREAT BOON TO THE Spirits I might have performed — to be in the position I was today.

I'd been Chosen by a strange and wonderful Lumani, Iomu. I hadn't known if I'd Bond with her or not, but the day of the attack at the Mists near Silverveil, her rather fanatical obsession with my size and strength had fused us into one and I'd become hundreds of times stronger. At the same time, I'd been blessed by the Spirits again: having met Feather, now Roo. I had never imagined any woman could be so accepting and instructive and passionate and... so full of love and life and joy.

Since then, I'd done many things my younger self would never have imagined. I'd travelled to the capital and met our queen and king as well as other Nobles and Royals. I'd even had dinner with the Royal family several times. And now, I was a part of a new Noble House and tomorrow would depart for Basia... now occupied by the feared Thraian Empire. My life had changed so much in a matter of a few weeks.

The twins, Falcon and Swift — who I'd known at Silver-veil as Agate and Tail — had arrived just a few hours ago. They'd had a chance to bathe and rest, even share one final meal with the Royals. Now the twins and Roo and Dawn and I sat in the common area of our suite.

My heart thundered with curiosity at what was to come. Roo had said she and Dawn wished to talk to me... and the twins... about our relationship. All I knew was, I loved Roo with all my heart and didn't want to ever let her go.

Roo and Dawn sat together on a smaller couch, while the twins occupied another couch and I sat in a chair. As with most furniture — built for people of a normal size and weight — the chair groaned as I sat in it. I hoped it wouldn't fall apart just yet.

Silence hung over us for a moment as we all looked around at each other a bit uncertain. Then Dawn looked to Roo, who spoke, a note of quiet command in her voice.

"Dawn and I have been talking. As we've told all of you, neither of us has been looking for a lasting relationship, for love." Then she smiled softly as she met the gazes of each of us three men. "But, you three have definitely made an impact on our lives. Dawn and I know that what we're about to do, going to Thraan, is a bit... crazy, and we don't want to force that upon you. We would like to know your reasons for coming with us, and how you feel about... us in general. But first, we'd like to let you know how we feel." She turned to Dawn.

The smaller, fair-skinned woman took a moment, perhaps composing her thoughts before she spoke. "I have begun to realize some things about myself." She was taking her time, seemingly thinking long and hard about her words before she spoke them. "Not that long ago, I told my Lumani that my heart would do exactly as I told it to do, that

I didn't want love. That was why I told you—" She looked up at the twins. "—I didn't want anything serious. I... was... afraid of love, I think; afraid of the heartbreak that comes when those who should love you, don't love you in the way you'd hoped." She drew in a long breath. Roo shifted a hand, laying it on one of Dawn's, supportive. Dawn's voice was heavy with emotion, a bit strained when she spoke next. "I realize now that I felt that way because of my parents and how I was treated as a child." She shook her head suddenly and with it seemed to shake off some of the heaviness weighing upon her. "And I don't want to live like that, cutting myself off from love, any longer." She met the twin's gazes, shifting back and forth between them easily. "I don't know how easy I'll be to love, what walls my heart still needs to break down. I don't know how well I'll love at first, either. But I'd like to start to find out." She pursed her lips for a moment as the fullness of her words sunk in. "Also... I come from a family where communal love was normal, and I don't think I will want to limit myself to just one man... or even two." With that her gaze flicked over to me and I felt a rather sudden bloom of heat upon my cheeks.

Was she suggesting what I thought she was suggesting?

I glanced at Roo, who was beaming with a wide smile, then winked at me. I wasn't sure I knew what that meant, and hoped they'd explain it soon enough.

Dawn finished with, "What I'm saying is, if you're going to be with me, you're probably going to have to learn to share me. And I, in turn, will be happy to share you." Her non-subtle gaze went from the twins to Roo and back. "If you're well with that, then I think we can move forward... together."

The twins, for their part, seemed a bit overwhelmed and confused by this. As caught off-guard as I was.

Dawn turned to Roo.

Roo sighed, a peaceful and calming breath, which somehow even made me feel a bit more relaxed. The radiant smile on her face was spread around to all of us, then she spoke. "I, like Dawn, have been... limiting my emotions with you, and now I would like to tell you why." She drew in another long breath. "I was married once."

Dawn laughed just a little at the stunned looks on our faces. I had to struggle to close my gaping mouth.

But as Roo told us the story of her husband Davas and how he had passed, I began to understand her better. She'd told me once that she'd also lost someone to the Dream Fever, just like I'd lost my mother and sister. I'd assumed a parent or sibling, but now I knew. And for the first time, I saw the mending fragility of this woman, who I thought to be so very strong and in control of her life and desires. When she'd completed her tale, she took a long look at each of us men and I warmed under the soothing embrace of her dark eyes.

You really love her, don't you, Iomu whispered within me.

I do.

But... you're curious about Dawn too, aren't you?

I... Luckily, I didn't have to answer that as Roo was continuing and I focused on her.

"I think you will understand why I might be hesitant to love again, so soon," Roo said. Then the clouds of melancholy upon her face parted and that sunny smile came out once again. "But I am learning that the heart wants what it wants. And though, I do not know if I love you as fully as I might wish to... someday, I know that I want you," she said looking directly at me. But then she turned to the twins. "And you, and you."

My heart sank a little.

She returned her gaze to me. "Rhino, Like Dawn, I am not certain I wish to limit my love to just one man. Our time together has been wonderful and I want more, so much more from you. And I want to give you so much more of me. I want us to be close. I want to build our relationship and know true love once again, with you." She smiled and suddenly any worries I'd had, any doubts fled. Even as she spoke her next words, I knew the truth of them. "But I have a large heart, and I may wish to love others as well." I nodded to this.

She rose and came to kneel by my chair, taking my hand. "But... since we already share a deep connection, I need to know how you feel about that, if you would be well with sharing me." She grinned with a flicker of a look back at Dawn. "I would be well with sharing you." She gave a breathy laugh. "You're big, there's a lot of you to go around."

I didn't know what to say to that, and Dawn spoke before I could form any sort of answer.

"There you go," Dawn said. "You know how we feel... how about you?"

The twins looked to me to respond first.

I turned to gaze into Roo's eyes as I considered everything she and Dawn had said. She was an amazing woman. All I knew in that moment was: "I don't want to lose you."

But could I be with her if she was with others?

She's amazing, you'd be a fool to turn her away, just because she's got too much love to give. Iomu was very opinionated about a lot of things. *And, she's giving you full rein to be with others... like Dawn. Don't tell me you haven't been thinking about that feisty Fey, I know you want to jump her bones.* Iomu could also be very crude, even though she'd had mostly female hosts before me.

I don't want to 'jump her bones,' as you say. But I couldn't deny the pull of Dawn's raw and powerful spirit. Still, she was even smaller than Ginea, I couldn't imagine we'd... *fit* well together.

I glanced over Roo's shoulder. Dawn was looking at me with unabashed interest. Whatever I felt, it was clear she wanted me.

So, what did I want?

Iomu was right, I would be a fool to lose Roo. And I knew Roo was right. She was overflowing with love and life, and I knew she would share that love with everyone she met, to some degree. I'd never have her entire heart... but I'd settle for having some of it, if it meant I had her in my life.

Exactly, Iomu said. *Now tell her that, then kiss her like you mean it. Then... perhaps we can ask Dawn to join us tonight?*

One thing at a time.

"I love you, Roo." I wasn't afraid to say it. "And I think I've always known I could never keep you to myself. I can feel it, your... immensity of love. You overflow with it. As big as I am, I know I could never be all that you need."

She blushed at that.

"And... I might be interested in exploring... what it means to... share." This with a quick, hopefully-not-too-suggestive look at Dawn.

Dawn winked at me.

I think I blushed then.

"Thank you," Roo said, and she reached out to pull me down for a soft, but lingering kiss. Then, as we drew apart, she whispered it again, a breathy benediction just for me. "Thank you."

I filled with heat and shivered at the true gratitude and dare-I-say love in her voice.

"What about you two?" Dawn asked the twins.

They looked at each other for all of a half a heartbeat

before grinning, the same smile on two faces. Falcon answered, "So you're saying we can be with you and Roo and in return, you and Roo will be with others like Rhino?"

"Yup."

Swift looked at me. "You promise you won't ruin them for us?"

"I promise, I'll be gentle," I said.

"Unless we ask him not to be," Dawn said quickly.

I *know* I blushed then, my imagination flashing the image of rough hard sex with the small woman and her loving every moment of it. Yeah, it was more than just my cheeks that heated this time. I swallowed hard, not able to say anything while Dawn winked at me, then laughed. Spirits! Was she crazy?

She wants to go to Thraan and make peace. So, yes, she's crazy, Iomu answered.

The twins laughed as well. "We know we can't compete with you for size, Rhino, but the two of us together are still something extraordinary. We'll make do," Swift said. Falcon finished with: "We're in... all the way."

"Yes!" Dawn said shooting to her feet. She went to the twins, kissing them each, saying: "Thank you for this. I promise this is going to be amazing."

"As for going to Thraan," Swift said as he rose. "Of course we will. As for why...? Because we'd follow you anywhere, to the ends of the earth and back."

I rose, grinning. "Count me in too." I looked at Roo. "Same reason."

Roo got up. "I will admit, I'm terrified to go, but you all are my family now, and I know, if we stick together, we'll be well." Her voice was just a little tremulous, belying her words. Then she took a breath and seemed to fill with resolve and certainty.

Dawn beamed.

Roo drew me apart from the others after this, bringing her hand to my cheek, her dark-eyed gaze capturing mine. I could see her devotion and respect in that one lingering look. "I think Dawn would like to be with you tonight," she whispered.

I knew it! Iomu cheered.

"And you'll... occupy the twins?" I breathed in return. I don't know why, but the image of her with the two of them — filling her front and back, making her scream with bliss — flashed across my mind. Oddly, I didn't feel jealous. If Roo was being given joy, how could I not love that?

You've got a dirty mind, Iomu said with a laugh. *But don't worry, so do I. I mean, what woman wouldn't want twins to pound her into oblivion one night and a giant to pound her back again the next?*

Whatever shade of blush had been on my face, I was sure I turned beat red then.

"You certain you're well with that?" Roo asked.

I nodded. "All I want is for you to be loved and cared for. It doesn't matter by who. I'm just glad I get to be a part of it."

She nodded. "I hoped you'd feel that way." She rose up to her toes, pulling me down for a soft and full kiss, which made that heat upon my face spread to all parts of my body.

I felt the strain and pain of my cock stiffening and bunching in my pants but tried to ignore it and focus on the wonder that was Roo.

Not long after that, we retired for the evening. The twins were excitedly chatting with Roo about everything they could try as they went to her room. Meanwhile my heart was pounding with equal parts doubt and desire as Dawn practically pulled me into my room.

Yet once the door was closed, she gave a bit of a laugh.

"Calm down, you big lug. It's not like you're a lamb headed to the slaughterhouse. Are you really that scared to be with me?" Before I could answer, she went on, voice softer, understanding. "Roo told me about your... betrothed and how you feel about... small women."

"Oh?" was all I could say. I didn't know whether I was horrified Roo had told Dawn about that... or relieved.

Dawn continued, "Yeah, and... frankly, I don't know what we'll be able to do, mostly I'm just curious about... you, and your... *size* and... yeah." She made it very clear — by running a finger over the bulge in my pants — what she meant by *size*.

Your cock, she wants to see your cock, Iomu purred. *So, take it out for her, show her that glorious slab of man-meat.*

I don't know what color I turned then, but Dawn's eyes went a little wide and she stepped back. "Rhino? Are you... well?"

Oh... come on, you big lug! If you won't then I will! Iomu surged up within me, taking control of my body. "Hello Dawn, I'm Iomu, Rhino's Lumani. I know what you want, but he's a little shy so, here you go." And just like that I was out of my clothes and standing naked before Dawn.

Then Iomu was stroking my cock. *You're not full yet, let's show her just how big you can be!*

I was mortified. *Iomu, no! You can't just take over my...*

My thoughts were cut off as I watched Dawn quickly strip out of her clothes as well, an eager smile on her face.

So... that had been what she'd wanted?

Oh.

Dawn hurried to get the bottle of oil on my nightstand, returning quickly to help Iomu stimulate me, pouring oil over my erection and helping to stroke it. Dawn was so small, and I so large, that when my cock was fully aroused, it came up to her chin!

All yours, Iomu said, returning control of my body to me.

I stopped stroking my cock, but the apology I'd been going to offer Dawn died on my lips. She was fully into this.

"You back?" Dawn asked looking up at me.

I nodded.

"Don't worry about anything, I'm not going to force you into anything and you're not going to hurt me. I just want to... have fun. Let's explore each other, shall we?" She said all of this with her two small hands around my cock, massaging oils into me.

What a woman.

"Thanks," I said. I'd needed that reassurance.

She stepped back then, pouring out a liberal dose of the oil over her body. "Now it's your turn to massage me," she said.

I reached out and ran two fingers down her arm, marveling at how large my fingers were compared to her. She shivered and shuddered at the touch, clearly more than a little worked up already.

And as if the floodgates were opened with that one touch, I allowed myself the freedom to do as she'd asked and hold her, caress her, massage her.

She moaned and sighed and quivered as I took my time spreading the oil over her. Her alabaster skin flushed a soft rose with arousal, her small breasts ever-so-sensitive to the rough caresses of my large fingers. And when she'd had enough of that, panting and mewling, she pulled my hand down to her core, where no additional moisture was needed. Two of my fingers filled her folds and quickly brought her to a screaming, shaking orgasm.

After that, we kissed and touched and played for a while.

Eventually, she said: "I am curious to see if you'll... fit in me." So we oiled each other up until we were both slick and slippery. I laid on my back. She was so small she couldn't even kneel on me, she had to crouch over me. Yet, try as we might, my cock only ended up slipping around and off her, not in. Yet, neither of us were frustrated, in fact we laughed through the whole ordeal. And at the end, she simply rubbed herself against my hard length, grinding her clit upon me until she came, all the while stroking me viciously, until I joined her in a powerful release. We made a royal mess, but neither of us minded. We'd not be sleeping on that bed again; we were leaving tomorrow.

We tore off the sullied sheets, and I curled up around her as she slept. As for me, some part of my heart — torn asunder by my experience with Ginea — healed that night. Love was love, and fun was fun, and Dawn — and Roo — were the perfect match for my soul.

CHAPTER 25

ROO

OH, BRILLIANT AND BLESSED SPIRITS! DAWN WAS RIGHT! Having the twins inside me, both at the same time, was blowing my mind. I couldn't stop coming.

They were standing, and I had my arms and legs wrapped around Swift, grinding myself down upon him as he rocked his hips in short thrusts up into me. Falcon was just as deep, driving into me from behind. Their strong hands supported me, and I felt weightless and free as those twin erections filled me, plunging deep. Falcon kissed my back and neck. Swift claimed my lips between my gasping breaths. Tears of pure ecstatic joy rained down my face as yet another hard orgasm shot through me, filling me with shocks of radiant bliss.

"Please!" I scream-gasped. "Please. Come!"

"Yes, goddess," the twins said as one, and instantly their thrusts grew rough and sharp, needful and raw. Swift buried his face in my breasts, grunting, sweat glistening on that beautiful brown skin. Falcon dug his fingers into my plump bottom and thighs, grasping me firmly as he sated his lust with savage strokes.

My orgasm redoubled its body-shaking bliss and exploded with an even more powerful release, even as the twins cried out and I felt their dual pools of heat blossom within me.

I shifted, throwing an arm back around Falcon's neck and pressed their heads down with my hands so I could have both of them buried in my bosom. And their kissing and sucking on my rigid nipples only added another layer of pleasure to this moment, as I shook through the completion of my orgasm. And when they'd spent themselves fully, they let me down slowly, though my legs were too wobbly to stand.

Then they bathed me, and themselves, from the wash-basin in the room, before laying me down on the bed between them to sleep soundly, exhausted.

Tomorrow our journey began, but tonight... had been an adventure indeed.

"I TOO GREW UP IN A SMALL FISHING VILLAGE IN THE EAST," Ceph said. The tall man had been accompanying me, never far away, since we'd left the capital four days ago.

Sensing emotions was becoming second nature for me as my spirit-gift developed. Leoa called it a gift of empathy. I'd been feeling Ceph's awkwardness and desire for me these past few days, so today I'd invited him to walk with me, starting a conversation. Once I'd done that, he'd opened up and had become a different person. He'd gone from awkward and reserved, to vibrant and alive with stories and a wide smile; his eyes sparkling instead of shadowed.

I liked to walk, despite that a carriage had been arranged for us. With the honor guard and a wagon train for all our things — Nobles had a lot of 'things' they travelled with apparently — we weren't moving that fast anyway. At this pace, it would take two weeks of travel before we reached the boarder. That just meant I had time to get to know Ceph and deepen my relationship with the twins and Rhino. It also gave me time to learn to fight.

Swift and Falcon were both skilled with weapons, but even their knowledge paled in comparison to Ceph, who'd been a Noble for more than seven years now and was well trained. Then there was the Guard Captain, a veteran non-True-Bonded man named Levin. And everyone's experience paled in comparison with Midnight, who was over a hundred years old, if the rumors were true, and still didn't look a day over forty. Apparently, Dawn would have many years of ageless beauty to look forward to as a Fey. So, every day before we broke camp, and every evening before we rested, Dawn and I and Rhino — and to a lesser degree Swift and Falcon — were drilled in weapons and hand-fighting. I was glad I'd started a bit of training with Dawn previously or I'd have been hopelessly left behind. As it was, I didn't take well to fighting. It was too violent and shocking for me. I hoped I would learn enough to defend myself if I needed to, while hoping I'd never need to. I did well with the hand-fighting, especially taking to the style which used an opponent's energy and movement against them, defensive and passive. I was also slowly picking up the bow and staff.

I kept the staff with me as a walking stick, while I walked and listened to Ceph.

He had a nostalgic, dreamy tone as he said: "My village's name was Anari-by-the-Sea or just Anarisea. It lay where the Anari, a distributary of the Elis River, met the Sea and it's a beautiful place. It's peaceful and pristine and lovely..."

He looked down at me with a shy smile. "Like you, Lady Roo."

I blushed at the compliment. I sensed his tension, the hesitant fragile emotions as he waited to see how I'd respond. I smiled as I looked up at him and decided to be direct. I'd always been one to say what I felt. It was time to get things out in the open. "You like me, Lord Ceph." Not a question, but he nodded.

"I've been taken with you since I first saw you," he said, honestly. "I have seen many beautiful women, but none have captured my heart like you, my lady."

He was earnest and sincere, and I could feel his attraction, the draw, the raw pull. It wasn't love yet, but I felt it could become so.

"I find you handsome as well," I said with a soft smile. I hurried on, saying, "However, if you wish to be with me there are things you should know."

He blinked. I was taking him by surprise being so forward, I felt his excited hesitation. He did want to be with me, but I guessed he hadn't thought it would be any time soon.

Having had this conversation once before, it came a little easier. "I am not a woman who will be bound to only one man. If you wish to be with me, you must accept that there will be others who are also with me."

I caught his glance over at Rhino.

"Yes, Lord Rhino is one of them."

I felt his fluctuation and fear. Probably that he'd never be able to compete with such a man.

"And if you were amenable to sharing, then you would both hold equal standing in my heart. It's not a matter of physical size or political influence or anything other than love. I sense you have a tender heart, and I believe we could be a good match. But I am a good match for others as well, and I am not limiting my love. If you wish to love me, that is the price."

He nodded, his emotions settled and he seemed to be considering. After a while he said: "It seems a fair price for one such as you. I don't doubt that other men would be drawn to you as I am. I believe I could share you with others."

"Good," I said, glad that had been settled. "And in turn, you'd be free to be with other women as well, I am all for sharing."

"Ah..." he said, drawing out the word. "I do not think I would wish to be with other women. Only you."

"I'm flattered," I said honestly. This was intriguing and good to know. I had thought most men would like the option to be with other women freely, but apparently Ceph wanted me, and only me. I was touched. I didn't ask if he had ever been with other women. It would be a boon if he had, since I wouldn't have to teach him. Instead, I turned back to our original topic.

"Tell me more about your village," I said, and he gladly obliged, happily talking about the various odd members of the town, some of its history, and other details. I drank it all in as I began to wonder... just how many men would wish to be with me? Between the twins, Rhino, and Ceph that was four already.

It is your spirit, which I think has only been enhanced by our joining and your spirit-gift, Leoa said. *You are a beautiful woman, but I believe men and women will be drawn to you more from sensing your peace and love and wishing to be near you. I do not know where it will end, you may need to start setting some boundaries and limiting your — let's call it — inner circle of love.*

Do you truly believe that? That I am so... captivating? I was aware of my physical charms, but I'd never thought of myself as special. It wasn't like I was the only woman with such a figure. But this, it seemed, went deeper. *When I first met Dawn, I was drawn to her, she was captivating. Are you saying I'm becoming like that?*

Yes Roo, you are. You are growing in your spirit daily and others are sensing it, as you did with Dawn's. But more, your presence isn't one of raw power, like Dawn, but of love and serenity and compassion, and I believe that will draw more people to you than are drawn to Dawn. I do not know what will happen when Dawn Bonds, perhaps she too will grow in spirit as you have, but for now, you are the more powerful in that realm.

Oh!

That... was something to think about.

And perhaps it was my distraction which made me ignore my own spirit-senses. I should have sensed the emotions of others around us, but I didn't.

It was only after a group of heavily armed men stepped out onto the road in front of us — and others, with crossbows, rose up from the ditches to either side of the road — that I sensed their tense anxiety. Yet everyone's emotions paled in comparison with the intense animosity and hatred I felt somewhere ahead of our group.

Then the first flight of bolts was loosed by the ambushers, and everything was panic and chaos.

CHAPTER 26

DAWN

I HAD NO WEAPON. I'D BEEN TRAINING MORNING AND NIGHT with various weapons but hadn't thought to keep any with me while travelling. We were still in Elista; we were safe. Or so I'd thought.

I'd been wrong.

And with no weapon, I had no idea why I was running toward the enemy and not seeking cover. I'd been in the front of our group, speaking with Midnight, when the attackers had surrounded us. The ones on the road ahead had had crossbows and already loosed their first volley. I'd managed to dive and avoid that round. After that, I'd figured I had a better chance in close with them than out in the open. At the very least some of them would have to drop their range weapons and that might save some of the others back at the caravan. But still, I wasn't sure why I'd chosen to charge instead of hide.

You are brash and bold. You do not run from a fight. I will do what I can to protect you, Amya said, still crouched on my shoulder. If I'd been Bonded, Amya could have taken control and used his knowledge to fight for me, but as it was, I wasn't sure how the tiny Lumani could help.

In the instant before I got to the attackers, I had the strangest thought: *running toward a fight is something my mother would have done. Perhaps I was more like her than I'd thought.*

Then I was among the armed men and had no more time for idle imaginings.

The man before me had dropped his crossbow and drawn his sword. He stabbed at me, his motion swift and smooth, well trained, but I'd been trained in avoiding attacks since I was a girl and I deftly danced out of the way of the strike, spinning inside his guard and with a quick dual motion of both hands disarmed him.

But I'd left myself open to his free hand, which was suddenly grasping my hair, yanking my head back. Since he'd dropped his sword, his other hand balled into a fist as he drew it back to strike. But I smashed my fist into his nose before he could hit me.

He yelped, nose gushing blood, and released me. I took that opportunity to knee him in the groin. He was armored, but that area was only protected by a loose chain skirt around his thighs and my leg drove up under that to connect with his precious parts.

He yelped again, doubling over. I grabbed the sides of his head with both hands and smashed it down into my knee. He reeled, staggering backward. I dove for his sword, and plucked it up. I got to him before he'd recovered and slashed across his throat. I wasn't well trained with a sword, but 'going for the throat' had been an early lesson. Though... I'd never actually done it before and the amount of blood that came spraying out was a bit unexpected, covering me head to waist.

I dropped the blade to try to wipe away the hot mess from my eyes, hearing men closing in around me.

Two on your right, one on your left, Amya warned. *Now only one on your right, no... none. Midnight is... amazing.*

Duck!

I threw myself to the ground and rolled, coming up in a crouch. I had most of the blood out of my eyes, but not all of it, and blinked, trying to clear my vision. A man was turning toward me, after — I'm guessing — having tried to remove my head. I couldn't see things clearly, but I caught enough to see he was slashing at me. I slipped to the side and snapped a kick up at his hand. I missed, but still hit his arm and knocked his sword away. Then gathering my legs beneath me, I surged forward with all my Fey strength and simply launched myself at him, hands out before me. I hit him mid-chest and managed to knock him back and down, landing on top of him awkwardly. It took me a moment to gather myself from my splayed-out landing and try to punch him, but in that time he'd also recovered. With my limited vision I didn't see his punch and a fist hit my face unexpectedly. I was knocked to one side, head ringing.

I flailed, lashing out with my legs, connecting with something, hearing a grunt of pain.

Then I heard Midnight's voice. "Stop thrashing so I can get you up!"

I did as instructed and was quickly pulled to my feet. There were other bits of fighting going on around us on the road, I could hear it. My vision was still blurry.

"Bleeding Pits! Swan! Get behind me." I heard from Midnight and was a bit confused as I felt her push me a bit. My name was Dawn not Swan.

Then I heard another voice. "Let me have the brat and I may let you live, Fey." It was harsh and female.

Suddenly my mind clicked. Swan! From my mother's tales of the old Royal House. Lady Swan had been involved with Merlin. She'd fled and... was never found afterward. Everyone thought she'd run to the northern wilds or Basia, and perhaps she had, but it seemed she was back now.

"Not Bloody likely," Midnight hissed.

I took the precious moment I had then, while I listened to this exchange, to clear my vision, mostly I felt like I was just smearing around blood and road-dust, but I was able to regain a bit more of my sight.

Then I heard... something. It was unlike anything I'd ever heard before and sounded like a scream, but far more intense, and extremely loud. Spikes of pain drove into my ears, then... I heard nothing. My head spun and I felt midnight fall back onto me as we both collapsed onto the road. I scrambled out from under the small Fey woman. Midnight was shaking her head: ears, eyes, and nose all bleeding. I still couldn't hear anything.

I think that was some sort of sound-based-scream attack. Amya seemed a bit dazed as well.

I looked down the road and saw a woman in armor, a breastplate, padding, grieves and bracers with streaming long blond hair, and eyes... eyes that drove a spike of fear into my heart. They were truly burning red, smoldering like dark flashing embers, as she snarled in rage.

She raised a hand toward me and I dove out of the way as a beam of harsh, dark-red *something* blasted at me. But in my scramble to get out of the way, I tripped over Midnight and tumbled, I came up too slow and Swan already had her hand pointed at me, I saw the growing red energy flash toward me...

Then someone was in front of me, taking the blast full on their back, pushing them into me, as we both fell over.

It took me a moment to recognize the face of the man lying on top of me.

...Eadric?

I tried to move but couldn't. Eadric had saved me, but was dead weight on top of me, limiting my movements. Then I saw two birds flash by overhead, a falcon and a swift.

I wiggled until I got an arm free, then started to push Eadric off me. He seemed to be alive, but given he'd taken the full force of that strange blast, I didn't think he'd live for long.

Yet his eyes snapped open as I grunted, pushing him up. He pushed himself up to his knees, still straddling me and gave a wan, weary smile. He said words I couldn't hear, then grimaced in pain.

"Get off me, we're in the middle of a..." I wasn't sure if I was speaking at the right volume, I couldn't hear myself, but even as I tried to speak, I looked around and saw the fighting had mostly stopped. I peered around Eadric to see Swan riding off on a horse, a few others following her, fleeing.

We'd won?

Yes, we won.

I was curious what had happened exactly, but for now, I was more concerned about Eadric. I extricated myself from under him and scrambled to my feet, pulling him around to look at his back. I was sure that strange energy attack should have destroyed him. It had seemed powerful enough to blast through us both. His clothes were gone, blasted away, and there was a large area of red, exposed muscle... and I think I could see some of the bumps of his spine. It was horrid, but still far better than what I'd expected.

Still, it was gruesome and with everything else that had

happened — blood still covering me — I chose that time to be sick on the road, losing my lunch and probably my breakfast. Once I was done with that, kneeling on the road feeling more than miserable, I reached up to touch my sensitive, stinging — and still non-functioning — ears. My fingers came away bloody.

I didn't think swans could make deafening noises, I said to Amya, partly as a question.

Their honk is loud and obnoxious, but not deafening, no. This was something else, and with those blasts of energy... it must be a spirit-gift of some sort.

Great.

I FELT UNSTEADY AND WEAK. I SAW A SHADOW APPROACH ON the road and looked up to see Falcon. He held me, helped me up as he spoke. I heard nothing. I pointed to my ears and shook my head, saying: "I can't hear anything."

I may have shouted, too loud. Falcon flinched back, releasing me. I collapsed again, legs like water.

Someone lifted me, carried me. I was dizzy and disoriented and didn't really know where I was or what was going on. I was taken to some place off the road and laid on a blanket. The next thing I was able to focus on was Roo, when she came to see me. She had a bandage around one arm but seemed well otherwise. She smiled down at me, and I felt her compassion and caring like a warm blanket upon me. I hadn't realized how concerned I'd been for her until I saw she was well. I felt myself ease then, releasing the bunched-up tension from the fight.

I must have relaxed enough to sleep, as I started awake at a loud ringing in my ear. At least I was hearing something, but it was painful and intense. Night had fallen, and someone was nearby. I could see well in the dark and saw Roo there, sitting next to me. But with her was the tall man who been smitten with her, the one she'd been talking to on the road: Lord Ceph.

He leaned over me and put his hands to either side of my face. Then I felt... something. It was extremely odd, like my body temporarily turned to jelly and sort of... shifted, shimmying around a bit, then was put back to normalish.

The ringing vanished, and I heard only the soft sweep of a night's breeze and the call of distant crickets.

"Can you hear me?" Ceph asked, softly.

I nodded. "Yes. What... did you do?"

"Hard to explain. I healed you, sort of, but you'll be weak and feel... odd for a while. Hopefully, it'll be gone by morning as your injuries were not severe."

"Thank you," I said, not fully understanding, but still grateful.

Ceph rose, saying to Roo, "I have others to attend to, but may I return to you after?"

She nodded.

He left.

"Got a new lover?" I asked, trying to be playful, but my voice was raw and hoarse and it came out as crass and harsh.

She smiled down at me. "We'll see." She lay down next to me, warm and close. "I was so worried for you, for...everyone. That was... horrible!"

Battle usually was.

"I'm glad you're well," I said softly.

"Ceph and Rhino were close by, they protected me. Rhino was... quite hurt, but Ceph was amazing." I felt her stroking my hair. "You should rest."

I sighed and nodded, I was so very tired and as Ceph had said, feeling... odd in a way I couldn't describe. Still, I closed my eyes and after a moment felt more peace and warmth flow into me, probably from Roo. Then I was fast asleep.

CHAPTER 27

ROO

Now, thoroughly exhausted and also thoroughly pleasured, I fell forward onto Ceph after our slow and quiet — and very satisfying — lovemaking. His long cock was still throbbing inside me with the aftershocks of his release. Bliss shivered through me with the remembered heights of my own orgasm. The night's breeze chilled the sweat on my back, but our bodies, pressed together, kept me warm.

"I've never... that was... you're... you're amazing!" he whispered.

As was he. He'd turned out to be well experienced, which had been a relief, since I'd not had the energy to teach him. "So are you, in love, and in war. I... you saved me today, thank you." I kissed him softly, and he responded, lips brushing and playing for a moment as he wrapped his long arms around me, holding me closer. We lay there, snuggling until our bodies cooled. Then he wrapped the other half of the large blanket we were lying upon around us and we slid to slightly more comfortable positions, my body still mostly covering his, pressed close, to sleep.

I woke to bright sunlight — I was facing east and the dawn was clear and bright — as I blinked my eyes open.

I must have groaned or moved.

"I love this time of day." I heard from behind me. I rolled over to see Dawn sitting, stretching, bright-eyed and smiling at me. "How was he?" she asked with a faint smile.

"Very skilled," I said with another it's-too-early-for-this groan. "How are you?"

Dawn nodded slowly, growing somber. "Better." She shook her head, and I felt fear and doubt creep into her, not emotions I associated with her.

"What is it?" I asked softly.

Her eyes were no longer bright, but hooded, when she said: "I did this." Her voice was soft. I was about to ask what she'd done, when she asked, "How many died yesterday?"

I had been with Ceph as he'd checked the injured. I still didn't really know what he'd done. He'd explained it as "manipulating their bodies to shift uninjured bits to the injured area and shift the injured bits to other areas." I had no clue what that meant and hadn't wanted to interrupt him to ask.

"Nine," I said softly. "Nine of our guard died with another two that probably won't be able to continue with us. Rhino and Midnight were also quite hurt as well."

"And it's all my fault," Dawn said softly. I saw a shiver take her. "That woman leading the attack, Swan, she's an old enemy of my mother's and she was after me. I'm sure of it. All those people died or were hurt for my sake."

Swan? I too had heard that name. When the queen had been telling tales of her past, Swan had been... a minor character, a lover of... Hale? Yes. And after everything, she'd been one of the few from the old Royal House who hadn't been found.

"Oh." It was all I could think to say.

I felt something bubbling up within me. With my spirit-gift, I identified the emotion quickly: hatred. Something I'd never felt before. But... I'd sensed it yesterday from someone nearby, and now... it sunk bitter talons into my heart. I hated Swan for what she'd done, for the attack and those who'd suffered because of it. Mostly, for what Dawn was going through now. I hated Swan, even though I didn't know her at all, hadn't even caught sight of her yesterday. And I hated that she'd made me feel this horrid emotion.

If I knew one thing, it was, "This wasn't your fault, Dawn. It was her fault. Don't blame yourself." I was a bit surprised at the venom in my voice. This was Swan's fault, and it had turned our world suddenly upside down. I had never had an 'enemy' before, never had someone trying to kill me. Experiencing it now, I felt this rawness within me, this anger and pain and hatred and it was so jarring, so anathema to my being that I was being thrown out of alignment, out of myself.

You are a being of peace and love, of course hatred is foreign to you, Leoa said, trying to be soothing.

So, what do I do about it? How do I get rid of it?

All emotions are fleeting. They come and go. This will pass. For now, remember those you love, focus on them, not the ones you... dislike. A very diplomatic way of putting it.

I focused on Dawn first. She was shaking her head. "But it *is* my fault. If I hadn't been in this group, she wouldn't have attacked us. If I hadn't insisted on going on this mission, leaving the safety of Silverveil and... Oh..." She'd realized something. "I knew it!"

I suspected I knew what conclusion she'd just come to. "The attack on Silverveil, at the Mists?" I asked.

She nodded. "It had to be Swan!" Her face darkened, lips

curling, bitter. "I knew it was my fault, all of this is my fault! I should have stayed far away, in foreign lands and never returned home!" She was shaking now, on the verge of tears. I'd never seen Dawn like this before, so uncertain and afraid. I rose, finding my clothes, and dressed quickly to go sit next to Dawn and hold her close. I knew this was Swan's fault. Even if Dawn had been her target, it was never the victim's fault someone attacked them. I tried to send soothing emotions into Dawn using my spirit-gift, but I couldn't; I was blocked. I was still so angry at Swan for doing this to my friend. So, instead I pulled Dawn close and held her tightly.

"I'm putting you in danger," she said softly. "All of them, Swift and Falcon, and Rhino and...Oh!" She broke free of my hold on her and surged to her feet. "Eadric! Where is he, did he survive?"

I blinked. There had been an unexpected additional member of our party after the fight yesterday. I hadn't really known him, but I did recall now that he'd come and comforted Dawn when we'd been sitting vigil over Swift. He'd been badly injured, but oddly seemed little affected by it. He'd even been the one to carry Dawn to where she was now before allowing anyone to tend to him. He shouldn't be far away.

He wasn't. Dawn caught sight of him quickly and lurched toward him, still apparently unsteady on her feet. I rose and followed her.

She knelt next to the man as he slept. Looking up at me, she asked: "The injury on his back, is he...?"

"He's well, Ceph tended to him in the same way he did for you. Don't ask me how, I still don't really understand it."

"Thank you," Dawn said, even though I hadn't done anything. I think she was still a little disoriented.

The man came awake when Dawn touched his face. He blinked, smiling up at her. "Hello Dawn. I... came to... I saved you. I love you." He seemed a little dopey, whether from recovery or just waking up.

"I love you too," Dawn said quickly, bending low to embrace him awkwardly and kiss him. "You saved me. We should be dead. I don't know how we survived."

He smiled, blinking, seemingly surprised at her attentions. "I... Bonded not long after you left Silverveil. I... I made friends with Falcon and Swift and found out about your plans and I thought I'd try to find you. I took a fast horse and travelled cross country. I caught up to you yesterday, just before the attack, then... I saved you." He blinked. "Who was that madwoman, and what was it that hit me? It hurt like the blazes."

Dawn let out a shuddering half-laugh-half-cry. "It hurt like... You should be dead! We should be dead. I don't know what that was, but..."

"I'm tougher now," he said softly. "My new name is Pangolin, an animal with a hard shell. I can take a hit or two."

"Apparently." Dawn pulled him close again. He was in an awkward half-sitting position, but didn't seem to mind, he put his arms around her, drawing her close. They held each other for long enough that I was beginning to feel awkward standing there watching them.

Dawn caught my gaze and let out another awkward laugh. "Ah... Eadric — no, sorry — what's your new name?"

"Pangolin. Call me Pan."

"That's going to take some getting used to. Pan, this is Roo, my dearest friend."

"A pleasure to meet you," I said with a nod. "And you have my deepest thanks for saving Dawn's life."

"And mine," Dawn said, now sitting in his lap as he sat up. "I'm so sorry Eadr—" She grimaced. "—Pan." She smiled at him, and he beamed back. He didn't seem to mind at all. "Thank you for coming for me," Dawn whispered. "After... everything I put you through. I was a wretch, and yet you still found me and saved me. I... I can't..." And she began to weep. Again, this was so unlike Dawn; even Pangolin seemed to think so. He looked a bit stunned at this reaction from her, but then, he just held her close and she fell into him crying on his shoulder.

I let them be for a moment, returning to Ceph who was just starting to rise.

"How are you feeling?" I asked. He'd had a tiring day yesterday, fighting, healing, then satisfying our mutual desire.

He smiled. "Radiant as the sun in the sky, now that you are here."

I blushed. No man, not even Davas, had been so poetic when speaking to me.

"I don't usually like sleeping on the ground, but last night, with you in my arms, was the best sleep I've had in ages." He rose, finding his clothes and dressing. There was blood and dirt on his nice shirt and breeches, he didn't seem to notice. "I should check on my patients, not that I'm much of a healer, but I do what I can." He shrugged. "Care to join me?"

"I... need a moment to myself, if that is well with you?"

He smiled and nodded. "Of course, Roo, I love you." He said it so matter-of-factly, that I didn't fully register his words for a moment. And when I had, I didn't know what to say. We'd had one night together, and barely a day of getting to know each other before that. My heart was still so uncertain. I knew I was fond of Ceph and our time together last night had been wonderful, but...

He didn't seem to notice my disorientation and drew close for a kiss on my cheek, then was off, whistling. I blinked, watching him for a long moment before I returned to myself, still no closer to understanding Ceph... or my own feelings in that moment.

I went to check on my friends. Rhino was sleeping. He'd been the worst off. He'd had no weapon but had used his great strength to fight the attackers yesterday, suffering many grievous injuries but somehow managing to stay on his feet until the last of the foes had fled. He was extremely tough, it seemed. Perhaps he had some of the protection of a beetle's shell, or perhaps he hadn't noticed the pain, lost in a frenzy. I didn't know. But he looked well enough now, if pale. Swift and Falcon were sitting, talking quietly to each other. Neither had suffered great injuries, both experienced enough warriors to deal with these foes. They smiled upon seeing me and let me know they were well.

After that, wanting to be alone, but not wanting to go far, I went to sit in the carriage. Both horses were dead in the traces. We'd not be using the carriage again, but for now, it was a private place to think.

I tried to calm my emotions, but they wouldn't settle. I'd taken Leoa's advice and gone to see those I loved, but still I felt so confused and so... enraged, which was so foreign to me, I didn't know what to do with it.

Breathe, Leoa suggested. *Long, deep breaths. I've felt anger many times in my many lives and you have been lucky to have lived so long and not experienced it. I hate to say it, Roo, but it will probably return. You'll need to know how to deal with it when it does.*

She was right. I tried deep breaths and that helped a

little... until my mind flashed back to the horridness of that fight: the blood and all my injured friends. And... "Argh!" I couldn't help but let out some sound of frustration and raw fury.

Breathe.

I am breathing!

Breathe deep, think of your home, the peaceful seaside. Think of those you love, remind yourself they are well now.

And they were, thankfully. *But... what happens when...* No, I couldn't even contemplate losing someone I loved, not again. I'd lost Davas and it had broken me. I'd only just come to accept new love in my life. It was slowly helping me heal from the loss of Davas, but... *What happens if I lose one of them?* I asked. Losing someone to disease or old age was painful enough; losing someone to an enemy, in a fight... was more than just distressing. It was infuriating, abhorrent, and repulsive to even contemplate!

Leoa sighed. *This is what I meant. It is possible you may lose someone you love to forces other than nature and when you do, you may feel this anger again. You must learn to...* she sighed again. *You're not going to like it, but you need to learn to accept it.*

Accept it? How? No. It seemed an impossible task.

Yes, Roo, accept it, because otherwise anger will destroy you. Mourn those you've lost, but don't hold onto the anger. If you do, it will tear you apart. When you accept your anger, you're not saying that things don't hurt, only that you're not going to let your anger control you. When anger controls you, you do stupid things. When you control your anger, you can think clearly and make good decisions on how you will move forward.

That — as much as I didn't like it — made sense.

I sighed out a heavy breath in a huff. Then I let out a yell of all my frustration and fury, before resuming my deep breathing.

Yeah, sometimes yelling helps too, Leoa said.

Dawn found me a moment or two later, Ceph not far behind her. "Are you well?" she asked. I could see the same question in Ceph's eyes.

I gave them a wan smile. "Just... needed to let out some emotions. I'll be well."

Ceph nodded and smiled. I could see the kindness and compassion in his eyes, he wanted to climb into the carriage and hug me, but he saw Dawn doing that and simply gave another nod before leaving.

Dawn, like some weary child, climbed up beside me, then oddly into my lap, sitting across it to hug around my neck, laying her head upon my shoulder. "I think we both need someone to hold us," she said softly. I wrapped my arms around her and we sat together in silence for a long moment. Dawn had been right, simply having someone there holding me did help. I continued my deep breathing and slowly, the anger faded. It wasn't gone, but I felt more myself.

"Who is Pan?" I asked. My curiosity over the odd, small man was at least one thing I could do something about.

She laughed softly. "I may have mentioned I was accompanied on my travels by another Fey, yes?"

I did seem to recall that. "It was him?"

"Yes."

"He was at Silverveil, I saw him a few times."

"He followed me there too. I told him I wanted a break, time apart and he respected that, but once he was Bonded, apparently he came looking for me."

"And thank the Spirits he did."

"Or I'd be dead, yeah." Dawn lifted her head from my shoulder and looked up at me. "Tell me I'm doing the right thing by going to Thraan, risking the lives of all these people?" A bit quieter she added, "risking my own life." I didn't have time to respond before she went on. "I've been in dangerous situations before, but I always knew I'd be fine. I'd never truly feared for my life... until yesterday."

I could understand that thought. I'd felt the same.

"I thought I could do anything," Dawn said softly. "Now...?"

I pulled her close again. "You are a miracle," I whispered. "You have broken every rule and done your own thing and always made the best of it. You have trusted your gut and instincts and they've never let you down. I think you're thinking too much about all of this." I certainly was. "Get back to your feelings, your connection, your purpose. What does that tell you?"

She nodded, head against my shoulder still. "You're so wise, Roo. I hope, when I'm Bonded, I'll be half as wise as you are."

"If you are, you'll be truly unstoppable," I said with a bit of a laugh. "A terror of radical wisdom!"

She laughed at that as well. It felt good to be laughing with her.

"Thank you," she said softly. "I needed that."

We stayed together for some time. The sun was well up when someone came to get us for the morning meal. We drew apart then, and Dawn stood in the carriage looking back at me. "I'm feeling better now, ready to take on the world again." She smiled. "Thanks to you."

I didn't say it, but I'd found some stability in my emotions through connecting with her, my dearest friend. "We'll take on the world together," I said.

CHAPTER 28

DAWN

Everyone was looking to me. Roo may have been the head of House Rat, but I was the de facto leader of this group. I looked over the assembled men and women. Midnight was recovering from the strange shout that had deafened me. To hear her tell it, Swan had let out a super-human scream, which had buffeted Midnight physically, disorienting and deafening her as well. She'd taken the brunt of it for me. She was pale, but seemed well enough now, thanks to Ceph's 'healing.' The guard captain, Levin, had a bandage on his head and one arm in a sling. He looked rough but had also been tended by Ceph and was on the mend. Swift and Falcon were mostly uninjured, Rhino and Pangolin were healing and pale — also 'affected' by Ceph's ministrations — looking just a little unsettled. I too felt it, just a bit... odd, as if I'd been taken apart and put back together wrong, but somehow also right. Roo and Ceph seemed tired and worn, but well enough.

I stood. "Midnight, do you think you can track Swan?"

She nodded. "I should stay with you though."

I shook my head. "No, I need you on her tail. We can't

have another surprise attack like that. If you can stay close to her and watch her movements you may be able to warn us of an impending ambush." I grimaced. "She may also decide to go after Mother. We just don't know what she's planning, and we need a spy on her. You're the best suited for it."

She nodded. "I should send a pigeon to your mother at the next village to warn her."

"We'll do that, you should head out as soon as you're feeling well enough, to catch up to Swan."

Midnight nodded. She rose and began to gather her things, listening to the rest of our plans as she got ready to leave.

"The rest of us will continue on. We have two horses remaining and two wagons of supplies. We'll re-rig the wagons for one horse each. At the next village, we'll let the knackers know of our horses here and send someone to salvage the carriage."

"I can try to conscript some men from the next village to join the guard," captain Levin said.

"No, I think the honor guard just makes us stand out. We'd either need a small army or we need to be less conspicuous. At the village we'll refit ourselves to look more like travelling merchants. We'll send a pigeon to the capital of Basia, to let the Thraian army know we're coming, we wouldn't want to surprise them. Hopefully they can arrange an honor guard once we're within their territory, but for now, we keep a low profile."

The captain nodded and the others seemed to accept this.

I sighed heavily. "And I don't want to feel as helpless as I felt yesterday ever again. I am going to redouble my training at morning and evening rests, I suggest everyone does the same. Without Midnight, Captain, you'll be leading us. Teach us how to survive."

He nodded to that. I could see the heaviness of his expression though. He had his own doubts about himself. He had lost far too many men, good men. I hoped that prompted him to rethink how he'd train us. We'd see.

"Finally, we're going to take a day to rest once we hit the next village. A warm bed and a good meal will help all of us and give us time to make ourselves look like merchants." And I planned to use that warm bed for more than just sleeping. I was desperately hungry for a release from the tension and lingering doubt and fear I was feeling. I needed a distraction.

"That's all, let's get to it." I clapped my hands and people began moving.

Midnight came to me as the others prepared for our journey. She laid a hand on my shoulder. "Your mother will never forgive me for leaving your side, but I believe you are right. Someone needs to find out what Swan is up to." She sighed heavily. "Just, take care of yourself, will you?"

"I will," I said solemnly.

"You're the child of Legs and Alvere. You have untapped depths of strength and cunning within you. Don't forget that."

"I won't."

She nodded and drew me into an embrace. "Good."

"Thank you, Ona Midnight, for... protecting me yesterday. I probably wouldn't be alive if not for you."

She smiled. "I do what I can. And while I'm gone, you'll have to start being me and saving yourself."

I hoped I could do that. I nodded.

She was off, vanishing into the morning and I felt — at

the same time — safer knowing she was on Swan's trail, and also suddenly exposed with her gone.

We were on our way before noon and ate a cold lunch on the move. We reached a village by early afternoon, but it was tiny with few resources, and there was a large town down the road, so we continued, travelling until after dark, to reach it.

We were all too tired to do anything but sleep that night. The next day we spent refitting ourselves to look more like a small merchant caravan. We purchased a covered wagon and more horses. Then we bought new outfits, which either went over armor or replaced it. I knew if it came to a fight with the Thraians, we'd have no chance, so better to seem the part of peaceful traders. We sent a pigeon to my mother, to let her know of the attack. Then we sent a second pigeon off to Basia and the dragon lord who'd taken up residence there. I hoped we'd be greeted civilly.

We stayed in town that night, and though Rhino and the twins offered, I elected to ask Pan to share my room. I honestly didn't know what would happen. I knew he felt strongly for me, but I'd been pushing him away for so long now. For my part, I was so very grateful he'd saved me but was still working on breaking down the walls around my heart and wasn't sure what I could offer him.

So, we sat on my bed and talked. I told him how I felt — which included feeling confused — about him and what I'd discovered about myself and having blocked myself from love because of my childhood.

He nodded, seemingly understanding everything. And when I was done, he spoke, soft, but sure of himself. "Dawn, I think I've always known you were... struggling with inti-macy." He laughed, a light and breathy thing. "I think part of my attraction to you initially was thinking I could somehow cure you of that with my love. I'm not as naïve now." He held out his hand, and I laid mine in his. He clasped his other hand over mine and rubbed it slowly. "And... everything I said that day we went to Silverveil still stands. I love you. Since then, I've seen my anger for what it truly was. I wasn't mad at you. You had never promised me anything. I had made assumptions and was mad at myself for... all sorts of stupid reasons." He looked me in the eye then, glancing up from our joined hands. "I want to be in your life, Dawn. That is what I know for certain. I love you and want to serve you, any way I can. And if my service is only ever to defend you, and nothing more, I accept that. But know that I'll always be there for you, no matter what."

His gaze never left mine as he waited for my response.

I blinked a tear from my eye. He seemed so... grown up, so mature now. I didn't know what at Silverveil had changed him, perhaps his Lumani? One thing that hadn't changed, though, was his stalwart devotion to me. More than what he'd just said, he'd shown me with his actions, saving me from Swan's attack, risking his own life. I saw the man in a new light now, and my barriers around my heart crumbled just a bit more.

"Thank you, Pan, for everything, for saving me, and for... for taking that time away at Silverveil. I can see it changed you. I will strive to be someone worthy of your love." I put my hand on the pile of hands we had between us already. "And... I would like to explore... more of a relationship with you." I didn't have to ask if he was willing. I knew he was. He beamed at my words.

I then had a talk with him about sharing. He accepted that I was a free woman and he'd be well with me being with others, though he only wanted to be with me. I felt honored.

I kissed him then and found out he was a rather amazing kisser. We simply kissed for a long time, our mouths merging deeper and deeper as our hands began to explore each other. And, when I was ready, flushed with the warmth of his insistent affections, I told him exactly how I wanted to be pleasured that night. And he showed me just how willing he was to serve, how attentive and patient he could be as I lost myself in a haze of his adoration and heated desire. It seemed he had been well taught by the pleasure-givers in Weijin; very well taught indeed.

CHAPTER 29

DAWN

Sixteen days later we crossed into Basia, now a province of Thraan. Since Elista and Basia had had good relations and open boarders there was little to mark the crossing other than a sign indicating the new nation. Though... there had been signs of increased military movement on the Elistan side of the border. House Grizzly was patrolling much more frequently now.

On the Basian — now Thraian — side of the border, there didn't seem to be any patrols. Instead, we passed more and more refugees heading out of Basia to Elista. They were haggard and worn, carrying heavy loads — probably everything they owned — on their backs or in small handcarts.

When we politely stopped a young couple to ask them what was happening in Basia, the answer was grim.

"We got out of the capital just in time. The conscription squads were everywhere. We had to hide in ditches and forests until we were far enough away to travel openly on the road. The dragon lord seems to be staying in the capital for now, not concerned about eastern Basia, thank The Great Maker!"

I thanked them, but their news hadn't done much to make me feel better. I was realizing I'd need one Pits of a good plan to navigate the rough seas of diplomacy I was heading into. We pushed on for the rest of the day, as the stream of refugees slowly dwindled. Most of us walked, leading our three wagons, moving slowly.

I was so preoccupied with making plans that I was not the first to see the large group of men on the road ahead. Rhino nudged me, and I looked up. One of the men was waving his hands, moving toward us.

"Captain," I called, and Levin stepped forward. He was well recovered, looking hale and healthy. He was the only official guard we had now. The two who'd been injured we'd left in that first town we'd come to. We were trusting in subterfuge, and a smaller group would draw less attention. "Go see who these men are."

He nodded and jogged forward. We stayed where we were as the captain met briefly with the other man — roughly halfway between the two groups — then returned to us. He wore an odd expression. "They say they are our honor guard, sent by the dragon lord, princess." Yet, I sensed some hesitation from him.

"But...?" I asked.

He shrugged. "I don't know. A feeling. We should be wary."

I nodded. "Thank you, captain." I found it odd that these men had come so far east so quickly. From the refugees we'd talked to, they hadn't noticed any eastward movement by the Thraians, yet. Something was up, I just didn't know what.

Roo came forward hurriedly. "They are... planning something," she hissed in a whisper. "I sense subterfuge from them." She grimaced. "Oddly, no aggression though."

Well, that was something. Still, it was clear we were probably walking into a trap.

We approached slowly. I surveyed the gathered men trying to figure out what they might have planned. Something about the large group of men didn't sit right with me, and it must have clicked for me at the same time as it did for the captain.

"Uniforms," we both said. An honor guard would have a set uniform, the colors of Thraan or the prince they served, but these men, as much as they had tried to seem coordinated in their dress, were a bit too mismatched.

"These aren't the Thraians we were meant to meet," the captain said.

"But then... who are they, and why are they pretending to be Thraians?" I hissed. None of this made sense. We stopped our advance, still far enough away that we might just be able to run from them. "Turn us around quickly!" I whispered and the order was quickly passed to the others.

Even before we had fully turned our group around, Roo had spun with a gasp, eyes wide. She seemed overwhelmed. Perhaps she'd sensed something behind us?

I looked, seeing nothing at first... then a massive form appeared on the road, materializing out of nowhere.

A dragon.

I gaped. I had no clue how something that big could have remained hidden, but I'd not seen any sign of it until now. It was too big to comprehend. One of its legs could have crushed a wagon with ease. The body was perhaps a hundred feet long and thirty feet wide, sinuous and sleek, even if it was mind-bendingly large. Leathery wings spread out from the flanks of the body and were currently flared to the sides. They must have been close to five hundred feet from tip to tip, easily able to shadow a small village. The tail tapered slowly from the body to become a long and waving whip, with fan-like fins along its length. The end of the tail was a cluster of twitching blade-like bones. The neck was long and thick, arching up in an 'S' shape to a head, covered with ridges and horns. The massive maw of the beast — filled with rows of long teeth — looked like it could easily swallow a horse whole. And mounted behind the head was a man, hard to see from this distance.

But then the dragon lowered its head over us and the man came into view, wearing heavy armor of a color designed to match the shimmering copper scales of the dragon.

"Hello, princess!" the man called out, laughing with the confident superiority of someone who knew they were invincible; who knew they'd won. We were trapped between him and those other men on the road. "Apologies, but your journey ends here."

Like The Pits it does! I strode toward the dragon. I should have been terrified, but instead I was filled with a righteous strength of purpose.

"Dawn, no!" Roo hissed.

What are you doing? Amya asked.

Facing my problems head on. I said, my inner voice just a bit wild.

Dawn, no. That's... oh!

I stopped as I felt what Amya had, the tremor of power and insight that filled me. Suddenly Amya's voice was that much clearer... nearer. *Dawn!*

I know.

I laughed — as crazy as that was — despite the massive beast before me. Not because I felt superior but because apparently, facing down a dragon was radical enough that...

...I had finally Bonded.

Don't miss the next book in the series!

Double Danger
Shadows Over Elista: Book Two

An empire of dragons and deception awaits...

Asha (now Roo), is facing her greatest challenge yet: a monstrous dragon, and the Dragon Lord who controls it, and there is little she or Dawn can do in the face of such power.

But this Dragon Lord isn't what he appears. The youngest Prince of Thraan, he's at war with his brothers and the rest of the Empire and can't let Roo and Dawn continue with their quest.

With their original plans dashed, new undertakings force these friends apart.

Dawn is sent north to find the mythic barbarian tribes of the tundra. With her are the stalwart Swift and vigilant Pan who've shown her she's worthy of love, and that perhaps she can let down the walls she built around her heart during her neglected childhood. But can she allow herself such luxuries in these turbulent times? And is she willing to risk letting someone in only to lose them?

Roo's journey is even more perilous. She must go into

the heart of the Empire: a cruel place of depravity and deception. She's only just begun to believe that loving again is possible, thanks to the boundless affections of the ever-ready Falcon, the dedicated Ceph, and the mighty Rhino, but is she willing to risk her heart once more after having lost so much already? Especially with the trials awaiting her, which will test her body and soul. For, if she fails... death is a very real possibility.